Topaz
in the Limelight

WE SPARKLE WHATEVER THE OCCASION

Topaz
in the Limelight

HELEN BAILEY

Illustrated by Bill Dare

Hodder
Children's
Books

A division of Hodder Headline Limited

Typeset in Baskerville by Avon DataSet Ltd,
Bidford on Avon, Warwickshire

Printed and bound in Great Britain by
Bookmarque Ltd, Croydon, Surrey

The paper and board used in this paperback by Hodder Children's Books
are natural recyclable products made from wood grown in sustainable forests.
The manufacturing processes conform to the environmental regulations
of the country of origin.

Hodder Children's Books
a division of Hodder Headline Limited
338 Euston Road
London NW1 3BH

For Christie and Jack Rochester.

Northern stars!

Chapter One

Topaz crouched at the door, peering through the keyhole.

'Why are we hiding in the broom cupboard?' asked Sapphire as she pushed aside mops and buckets.

Topaz had been walking down the corridor with Ruby and Sapphire when she had pushed her friends into the cupboard and dived in after them.

'I'm avoiding Miss Diamond,' whispered Topaz. 'She's coming down the corridor.'

As Miss Diamond walked towards the broom cupboard, the three friends could hear the clickety-clack of the strings of beads around her neck as they bounced upon her ample bosom.

'I thought she wanted to see you the moment you got back to school this term?' whispered Ruby.

'She might want to see me, but I don't want to see her!' said Topaz.

Topaz wasn't sure whether Miss Diamond, Headmistress of Precious Gems Stage School, had discovered that last term she'd been the voice-over in a Speedy Snax Noodle Burger TV advert, without Miss Diamond's permission. If the Headmistress did find out, she'd pull Topaz's scholarship and she'd have to leave Precious Gems and go to Starbridge High.

Topaz groaned. 'I wish I'd never done the wretched advert,' she said, peering round the door. 'It's just not been worth the worry.'

The sound of Miss Diamond's clacking beads disappeared into the distance. The coast was clear, so they tumbled out of the broom cupboard into the corridor and began to walk to their first lesson.

'If you were going to worry about the advert so much, perhaps you shouldn't have done it?' said Ruby.

'I know that *now*,' retorted Topaz. 'From now on, I'm going to be a perfect pupil. The thought of being found out has been like a black cloud hovering over my head all holidays and it's even worse now I'm back at school. I'm just waiting for Miss D to come up behind me at any moment and say—'

'Could I have a word with you?' the familiar voice of Miss Diamond boomed down the school corridor as she marched towards them.

The girls stopped in their tracks and Topaz felt a sort of sick, sinking feeling in the pit of her stomach.

I'm doomed! she thought. *Any moment now I'm going to have to go back to my locker, pack my dancing shoes and leave stage school.*

She shuddered when she thought of the bully Kylie Slate and her gang, jeering when they saw her at Starbridge High.

Topaz turned around, ready to face Miss Diamond, when the Headmistress said, 'Sapphire, could I have a word with you?'

Sapphire tucked her long blonde hair behind her ears, smiled at Miss Diamond and said, 'I'm not in trouble, am I?'

Topaz kept her head down in case Miss Diamond saw the look of relief in her eyes.

'Not at all, Sapphire,' said Miss Diamond. 'Rupert, your mother's assistant, telephoned me this morning. She's due back in Starbridge this afternoon and she's asked to see you.'

Topaz's heart leapt. Sapphire's mother, Vanessa Stratton, was an international star of stage and screen, and other than in magazines, at the cinema or on television, Topaz had never seen her. Perhaps this would be her chance to meet a *real* star.

'Will she be at home?' asked Sapphire.

Miss Diamond shook her head. 'I'm afraid Rupert

says there isn't time. She'll be at the airport. A car will collect you from school at half-past three.'

Sapphire bit her lip. She couldn't remember the last time her mother had been back to their house in Starbridge Hill.

'Thank you for telling me,' she said, giving the Headmistress a hollow smile.

'Phew! That was close!' said Topaz as Miss Diamond disappeared into her study. 'I was *sure* it was me she was after.'

'I wish it *hadn't* been me,' said Sapphire. 'You can't believe how boring it is to sit in a VIP lounge, reading magazines and eating peanuts whilst your mother signs autographs and poses for photos.'

'How can that be boring?' said Topaz, who couldn't think of anything more exciting than having a mother who was a film star. Her mother, Lola, had to support both of them by working all hours, cleaning houses and offices.

'Why don't you both come?' said Sapphire. 'I could do with the company.'

'Oh yes!' gasped Topaz, thrilled at the chance of meeting Vanessa. 'That would be brilliant!'

'Don't you have an extra dance class after school?' Ruby asked.

'I'll skip it,' said Topaz. 'No one will even notice I'm missing.'

'I thought you were going to be the perfect pupil from now on?' said Sapphire.

'Starting tomorrow,' said Topaz. 'From tomorrow I *promise* I'll be the perfect pupil.'

An enormous black limousine with darkened windows pulled into Stellar Terrace and stopped at the bottom of the steps to the school.

'Is that for us?' gasped Topaz.

It had taken two terms for Sapphire to admit that she came to school in a chauffeur-driven car, but as she always made the chauffeur drop her round the corner from the school, Topaz had never seen it.

Sapphire shook her head. 'That's *nothing* like the car that brings me to school!' she laughed.

Whilst Sapphire scanned the road looking for a car she recognized, the front door of the limo opened and a man wearing a grey uniform and a peaked cap waved at Sapphire. It seemed the car *was* for them, after all.

'Oh no!' groaned Sapphire under her breath, blushing a deep shade of red. 'It *is* for us. How embarrassing!'

Topaz didn't think that having a huge stretch limo pick you up after school to take you to see your film-star mother was the slightest bit embarrassing.

'This is Parks,' said Sapphire as the chauffeur opened the door and the girls clambered in the back.

'Hello, Mr Parks,' said Topaz brightly.

'Just call me Parks,' said the chauffeur.

'He's not really called Parks,' whispered Sapphire. 'Mum calls all the chauffeurs Parks so she doesn't have to try and remember their names.'

After a moment, Sapphire asked Parks, 'What's with the car? We don't usually have one like this!'

'Your mother wanted you to make an entrance at the airport in case there were photographers around,' he replied.

'It's ridiculous,' moaned Sapphire.

'It's fabulous!' gasped Topaz as she slumped down in the cream leather seats and stretched out her legs.

The inside of the car seemed bigger than her bedroom. There was a television screen and a leather box full of cut-glass decanters and glasses that chinked gently together as the car pulled away from the kerb. Topaz was a little disappointed that the car had tinted windows. She could see out, but no one could see in. She *wanted* people to see she was in a stretch limo.

What's the point of swanning around in a posh car if no one can see you? she thought as they passed a bus shelter swarming with girls wearing the grey uniform of Starbridge High.

Kylie Slate was leaning against the bus shelter,

chewing gum, her face set in a permanent snarl. Beside her stood Janice Stone, who had once been Topaz's best friend, looking miserable. Kylie Slate waiting for a bus whilst Topaz was in a stretch limo! This was too good an opportunity to waste! Topaz opened the window and as the limo swept past she hung out of the car, waving at the bus-stop mob who stared open-mouthed.

As the car purred towards the airport, Topaz and Ruby couldn't help but notice that Sapphire looked unhappy.

'What's wrong?' Ruby asked. 'Aren't you looking forward to seeing your mum?'

Sapphire shrugged and let out a long, deep sigh. 'I suppose so,' she said. 'I'm just fed up that I never spend any time with her. The only time I see her is in magazines, on television or at the airport. And she only tells me she's in Starbridge at the last minute.'

'When did you last see her?' asked Topaz.

Sapphire stared out of the window and tried to remember. Her mother had been on a yacht somewhere hot for most of the previous summer, and away filming a mini-series with lions at Christmas. Then there had been the beach holiday which had lasted for weeks, a film shoot in a ski-lodge in the mountains and another holiday just to recover from filming in the ski-lodge.

'But Mum, how can you be exhausted from skiing when you didn't actually ski?' Sapphire had asked when her mother had called her to tell her she wouldn't be home for the Easter holidays because she had found the ski-slopes exhausting, and needed some time in a health spa to recover.

'Darling, the part called for me to look as if I could ski. It really took it out of me, putting those ski boots on several times a day. I'm more used to kicking off my high heels!'

Sapphire turned to look at her friends. 'I don't *know* when I last saw my mother,' she said. 'Topaz, you don't know how lucky you are. Your mum is *so* lovely.'

When the car finally pulled up to the kerb at Starbridge International Airport, the limo was so long it stretched from the door marked 'Departures' to the door marked 'Arrivals'.

Topaz was so excited that, without waiting for Parks to help, she flung open the door of the limo and scrambled out. There was a loud thud, a strangled cry and a straw donkey and a sombrero hat came flying over the top of the car door. Behind it, someone crashed to the pavement in a crumpled heap. Topaz could just see a pair of pink and white trainers sticking out from under the door.

'I'm so sorry!' cried Topaz, picking up the straw donkey and the sombrero from the road and peering round the door as Ruby and Sapphire rushed out of the car to help. 'I didn't realize there was anyone there! Are you hurt?'

A blonde girl sat on the pavement, hunched over her grazed knees. In the distance a woman could be heard shrieking, 'Don't worry, Princess! Mummy's coming.'

Topaz heard the voice and her blood ran cold. It couldn't be, could it?

The blonde girl looked up, saw Topaz and screamed. Topaz felt like screaming too. The person she'd knocked to the ground when she'd opened the car door was none other than Octavia Quaver from rival stage school, Rhapsody's Theatre Academy.

Octavia's mother, Pauline, appeared on the scene, huffing and puffing and pushing a trolley overflowing with suitcases and carrier bags.

'Mum, it's that girl!' wailed Octavia. 'She's got it in for me! Look at my knees! The catalogue won't want to use me for the photo-shoot now!'

A tiny trickle of blood had begun to run down Octavia's shins.

'You!' bellowed Pauline Quaver, her peroxide-blonde

hair quivering with rage. 'Are you determined to ruin my daughter's career?'

Pauline Quaver didn't give Topaz a chance to answer. 'A few days before Octavia has a modelling job for the Fin and Flipper swimwear catalogue and now look at her! They probably won't use her and it's all *your* fault.'

'It was an accident!' protested Topaz. 'She couldn't see where she was going with that huge straw donkey!'

Pauline Quaver's eyes narrowed. 'Are you saying this accident is my daughter's fault?' she hissed. 'Because if you are . . .'

Ruby reached into her bag and handed Octavia one of the cotton hankies her mother insisted she take to school. 'It's just a scratch,' she said. 'I'm sure it looks worse than it is.'

Octavia snatched the hanky and glared at Topaz. 'Are you stalking me?' she snapped. 'Everywhere I go, you seem to turn up!'

'Stalking *you*!' Topaz snapped back. 'As if!'

'Then what are you doing here?' said Octavia. 'And what are *you* doing getting out of a limo?'

Before Topaz had a chance to answer, Pauline Quaver, who had been making a big fuss of dabbing Octavia's scuffed knees, snarled, 'I may have to consult lawyers about this. We could be entitled to some compensation!'

'I think I'm going to faint!' squeaked Octavia.

'Oh, for goodness' sake,' said Sapphire. 'It was an accident and it's just a scratch. Stop whining.'

Pauline Quaver looked up at Sapphire with a crimson face and exploded with rage. 'How *dare* you talk to my daughter like that! Just who do you think you are?'

Sapphire looked at Pauline Quaver, tossed her golden hair and said coolly, 'I'm the daughter of an international film star. Who are you?'

Chapter Two

'That was brilliant!' said Topaz, giggling at the shocked look on Pauline Quaver's face as they left mother and daughter sitting on the pavement outside the airport terminal. 'I thought Octavia's mum was going to burst!'

'It was a *bit* mean of me,' said Sapphire. 'I don't usually do that sort of thing, but I'd had just about enough of that whingeing gruesome-twosome.'

'I almost feel sorry for Octavia,' said Ruby. 'She doesn't stand a chance of being a nice person having a mother like that.'

'Sorry for Octavia!' gasped Topaz, pulling a face. 'Those two deserve each other!'

The girls zigzagged through the chaotic crowds of

holiday makers, runaway luggage trolleys, business travellers, screaming children and people who just seemed to be hanging around, looking either bored or nervous.

'Which airline is your mum flying with?' Topaz asked Sapphire as they passed rows of check-in desks heaving with irate passengers.

'Mum doesn't fly commercial,' Sapphire replied, stopping outside a plain door on which a tiny brass plaque announced: VIP LOUNGE. She pressed a buzzer. 'The film company provides a private plane.'

Topaz was *very* impressed. 'Does she *always* fly in private planes?' she asked.

Sapphire shook her head as the door clicked open. 'Oh no. Sometimes she goes by helicopter.'

Outside the VIP lounge was a scene of confusion and chaos, but beyond the door with the brass plaque lay an oasis of calm. Harp music floated through air which smelt of expensive perfume as shiny air hostesses with immaculate make-up and wide toothpaste-white smiles glided silently across thick cream carpets, carrying trays of tall-stemmed glasses fizzing with champagne. One of the air hostesses smiled at Sapphire and nodded towards a sofa, across which was draped a woman with high cheekbones and expensive blonde highlights. She was holding a glass of champagne in her perfectly manicured hand, whilst around her a small crowd of people watched her every move, laughed at her jokes and re-filled her champagne glass whenever she took a sip. The woman looked every inch a film star and was unmistakably Vanessa Stratton.

Topaz was relieved to see that Vanessa looked *exactly* as she did in photographs. Celebrities could be *so* disappointing in real life. She remembered meeting Wendy Whisk when they were on the TV game show, *Proof of the Pudding*, and thinking that Wendy didn't look *anything* like she did on television, probably because she'd applied her make-up with a trowel.

'Look, everyone!' Vanessa announced to the lounge. 'This is my daughter, Sapphire! Isn't she gorgeous? Don't we look alike?'

Vanessa Stratton got up from the sofa, threw her arms around Sapphire and then gently pushed her away. 'Don't smudge my make-up,' she whispered. 'It's taken hours to look this natural.'

A small, anxious-looking man fluttered around the sofa, moving bowls of peanuts and tidying magazines into neat piles.

'Your daughter!' he twittered. 'I always think of you as sisters!'

Vanessa giggled as she sat back down. 'Oh, Rupert! You say the sweetest things. I'd be lost without you.'

Rupert gave a forced little smile. He didn't believe for one moment that Vanessa and Sapphire could possibly be sisters, not unless you had something *seriously* wrong with your eyesight, but fake flattery was part of being a film star's assistant and Rupert was a very good assistant.

Vanessa noticed her daughter hovering awkwardly by the arm of the sofa. 'Come and sit down, darling,' she purred, patting a cushion. 'Tell me what's been happening.'

As Sapphire went to sit down, Vanessa spotted Topaz and Ruby, who had been standing behind her daughter. Before they had a chance to say hello, Vanessa Stratton's eyes narrowed and she said in a steely voice, '*Who* are these people and *what* are they doing here?'

'This is Topaz and Ruby,' said Sapphire. 'My friends from Precious Gems.'

Vanessa looked Topaz and Ruby slowly up and down. She pointed at Ruby and wrinkled her nose. 'A little style tip,' she said in a voice mixed with disgust and pity. '*Never* wear claret with your colouring. It's a *big* mistake.'

'Mum!' gasped Sapphire. 'That's our school blazer!'

Vanessa gave a dismissive shrug of her shoulders.

'But she's not in school, is she, darling?' she said. 'She's in a VIP lounge.'

Ruby blushed and began to chew the end of one of her plaits. With her red face, red hair and deep red blazer, she looked like a large over-ripe tomato. Topaz hoped Vanessa wouldn't comment on *her* blazer, which was not only the wrong colour, but was a boy's blazer. She was still wearing a hand-me-down until her mum could afford to buy her a new one.

'Darling, it's lovely that you have made friends,' said Vanessa, taking another sip of champagne. 'Just make sure they don't get in any photographs.'

A large, greasy-looking man, dressed in a navy blazer with gold buttons, appeared in front of the sofa and did a sort of bow. Topaz noticed he had only three strands of grey hair plastered across his shiny, bald scalp.

'Miss Stratton?' he said, holding out an expensive-looking pen and a piece of paper. 'Sir Basil Speedy – owner of more than three hundred and fifty Speedy Snax fast food outlets. Could I trouble you for your autograph? I've been a fan of yours for more than twenty years!'

Topaz noticed Sapphire's mother wince slightly when the man said 'twenty years', but she nevertheless smiled sweetly, took the pen and paper and said, 'Of course! Would you like me to make it out to anyone special?'

The man turned crimson, and, sweating slightly, stuttered, '"To Basil with love from Vanessa" would be splendid.'

Topaz wanted to rush up to Sir Basil and say, 'I'm in one of your adverts, I'm the Speedy Snax Noodle Burger voice-over girl,' but decided against it.

Vanessa handed over her autograph and Sir Basil Speedy, hard-nosed, mega-rich businessman and international fast-food tycoon, skipped away like a young boy who had been given a new toy.

Topaz gazed at Vanessa in awe. She couldn't wait for the day when people would ask for her autograph, send over champagne and arrange for private planes to whisk her from one film set to another.

I must keep practising my autograph, she thought, as she tossed a handful of peanuts into her mouth.

Sapphire sat awkwardly by her mother's side, saying nothing.

One of the air hostesses approached, looking embarrassed, and handed Vanessa a card.

'Madam, I'm *so* sorry,' she said. 'There's a man

outside who has asked whether he could come in and do a short interview with you. We've told him to leave but he won't. He said if you knew he was here, you'd see him.'

Vanessa glanced at the business card the woman had handed her. It was from Tom 'Scoop' Mackenzie, chief show business reporter on *The Starbridge Gazette*. She'd known Scoop for years and could always rely on him to give her a good write-up and take a flattering picture, with plenty of airbrushing if necessary. She clicked her fingers and Rupert instantly appeared, holding a mirror. Vanessa looked at herself, patted her hair, licked her lips and said, 'Let him in.'

'Scoop, darling!' Vanessa gushed as a small man wearing a beige mac walked into the lounge. 'I'm very short of time, but when I heard it was you . . .'

'Thanks for seeing me,' said Scoop, flipping open his notebook and licking the end of his pencil. 'I won't keep you. Just a few facts, quotes and a quick snap and I'll be on my way. You're flying out to film *A Heavenly Match*, based on the blockbuster novel by Anastasia Draper.'

Vanessa gave Scoop a sweet smile and nodded. 'Directed by Joshua P. Finkleberg, the finest director in the business.'

Scoop started scribbling in his notebook. 'And you're playing Sister Ursula, a nun running an orphanage who falls in love with Father O'Leary, a priest played by Jake Lush. Is this your most important role yet?'

Vanessa lowered her eyes and looked up at Scoop through spidery false eyelashes. 'Oh no,' she purred, 'my most important role is to be a mother to my daughter, Sapphire.'

Scoop continued to scribble notes on his pad as Sapphire fiddled with her hair and shifted uncomfortably on the sofa.

'It must be very hard for you to have to leave your daughter for weeks on end,' said Scoop. 'How do you manage?'

Vanessa wiped away an imaginary tear and put her arm around Sapphire, who stiffened. 'Scoop, you have no idea how hard it is for a mother and daughter to be parted. But we're on the phone to each other several times a day, aren't we, darling?'

Sapphire said nothing. A red flush began to creep up her neck. Topaz and Ruby noticed her normally composed face begin to take on a slightly twisted look.

Scoop Mackenzie closed his notebook and began to get his camera out of his coat pocket. Unlike some film stars he'd interviewed, however many champagne cocktails she'd drunk, Vanessa Stratton only told you what she wanted you to know and no more. There were no surprises when you interviewed Vanessa and today had been no exception. He hadn't wanted to make the trek out to the airport, but it had been a slow news day and the editor needed something for the front page. If he took a photograph and got the picture desk to enlarge it, that would fill up some extra space.

Suddenly, there was a commotion on the sofa.

'Don't believe her!' yelled Sapphire, breaking free from her mother's embrace and jumping to her feet. Tears flowed down her cheeks. 'She never phones me, she's never here, she doesn't even know the names of my school friends! She's not how a mum is supposed to be!'

Sapphire turned to her mother, her face contorted with a mixture of hurt and anger. 'Why?' she cried. 'Why can't you be a proper mum? Why do I never see you? Why did you and Dad send me to stage school when you know I want to be a doctor? Why? Why? WHY?'

The lounge fell silent, except for the sound of Sapphire's sobbing. Topaz longed to go over and put her arms around her distraught friend, but everyone in the lounge seemed frozen with embarrassment.

Vanessa saw the startled expressions on the faces of those around her. This was *very* awkward.

She noticed Scoop Mackenzie had reopened his notebook and had his pencil poised. What else might Sapphire say? She could just see tomorrow's front page in *The Starbridge Gazette*: Sorry Sapphire Sobs: 'I never see my mother,' next to a picture of her hysterical daughter. Vanessa shuddered at the thought. It wasn't that she didn't want to see her daughter – of course she did, especially when photographers were around. Sapphire was very photogenic and in the right light, with carefully applied make-up and a good photographer, it was just possible that they could be mistaken for sisters. But what with film-shoots and parties, hair appointments and holidays, there was never the time to go home, unless of course it was for a photo-shoot. The Starbridge Hill mansion photographed *so* well. It had looked *wonderful* in the last edition of *Celebrity Pools & Patios*.

'Darling,' Vanessa purred, just loud enough for everyone to hear, 'I know I've been far too busy lately, and I hate myself for it, I really do. Can I help it if I'm in demand? But you know I'm always thinking of you, and Nanny Bean looks after you as if you were her own daughter.' Vanessa smiled weakly at those around her. No one smiled back. Not even Rupert.

Sapphire had heard it all before. She slumped back down on the sofa and hugged her knees.

'I'm so fed up of never seeing you, Mum!' she said,

her voice trembling. 'All I get is five minutes in an airport eating peanuts and being bored whilst you sign autographs and play the star!'

Vanessa looked at the horrified faces around her and took a big gulp of champagne. Everyone was staring at her, *especially* Scoop Mackenzie. This called for a grand gesture. She'd have to think fast.

'Sweetheart!' she announced in a loud voice. 'I didn't want to tell you in front of the press but I've been planning a surprise for you and your friends. I'm flying you all out to Palm Island on a private jet to join me on the film set, *and* I'll make sure you all have a part in the film!'

A murmur of 'How lovely!' and 'What a wonderful surprise!' rippled around the lounge. Vanessa lunged towards Sapphire and put her arm around her surprised daughter. Topaz, who had quietly been trying to count how many peanuts she could get in her mouth at once without swallowing, practically choked as there was a flash and Scoop Mackenzie captured the moment in a photograph.

One of the shiny air hostesses appeared by the arm of the sofa. 'Captain Dales would like to welcome you on board and is ready for take-off at your convenience,' she said.

Rupert went into a flap and began fussing around, picking up bags and double-checking their passports.

Vanessa applied another coat of lip-gloss and smoothed her hair as Sapphire remained forlornly by her side.

Topaz couldn't bear it any longer. The moment Vanessa got up from the sofa, she rushed over to sit next to Sapphire.

Vanessa paused by the door. 'Rupert, I'm sure I've forgotten something,' she said. 'I just can't think what.'

She looked around and noticed Sapphire's tear-stained face. *Oh, that's what it is!* she thought to herself. *I've forgotten to say goodbye to Sapphire!*

As she rushed back and swooped to give Sapphire a parting kiss, Topaz heard Vanessa hiss at her daughter, 'How *could* you show me up?'

Chapter Three

'Topaz, what *are* you doing in this picture?' asked Miss Diamond, pointing at the front page of *The Starbridge Gazette*.

They'd been about to start an IT class when Miss Diamond had put her head round the door and called Topaz and Sapphire into the corridor.

'Choking on a mouthful of peanuts, Miss Diamond,' said Topaz, peering at the newspaper. She'd dreamt of having her picture on the front page of *The Starbridge Gazette*, but this *wasn't* what she'd had in mind. It looked as if she was being sick behind the back of the sofa.

'I mean,' said Miss Diamond in an icy voice, 'what were you doing at the airport in the first place? Didn't you have a dance class after school?'

'I asked Topaz and Ruby if they could come with me,' said Sapphire quickly. 'I'm sorry. I felt I needed my friends there.'

The girls took a closer look at the newspaper article. A tear-stained Sapphire was pictured hugging her mother, with Topaz spluttering in the background.

NICE ONE, MUM!

Star's Surprise for Daughter

There were emotional scenes at Starbridge International Airport yesterday as film star Vanessa Stratton was briefly reunited with her daughter, Sapphire, before jetting off to Palm Island to film A Heavenly Match, based on the blockbuster by Anastasia Draper. In an exclusive interview, Vanessa told our ace reporter, Scoop Mackenzie, about the difficulties of juggling a career as an international film star and being a mother.

'I'm a mother first and a film star second,' said Vanessa, clearly upset that she would be parted from her daughter for a few weeks. 'We speak on the phone several times a day and I always make sure I am back for important events in Sapphire's life. We're more like sisters than mother and daughter.'

The lovely Sapphire, who has inherited her mother's stunning looks, added, 'The most important thing is that I know that my mother is always there for me and does everything she can to see me as often as possible.'

And just to show how much she misses her daughter, Vanessa revealed to The Starbridge Gazette *that she would be arranging for her daughter and some of her daughter's friends to join her in Palm Island on the set of* A Heavenly Match, *where they would be given roles in the film.*

'I've had many important roles,' said the ever youthful star, 'but that of being a mother to my daughter is the most important role of my life.'

'I didn't say any of that stuff,' said Sapphire sourly. 'It's all made up to make my mum look good. I bet she didn't even think of arranging that trip until the last minute.'

Miss Diamond took the newspaper back and sighed. 'I'm sorry, Sapphire. I'm afraid I can't allow you to leave school during term-time.'

'Oh no!' gasped Topaz, seeing her chance of being in the film disappear. 'I mean,' she said, noticing Miss Diamond's raised eyebrows, 'it's really disappointing for Sapphire.'

Miss Diamond turned to Sapphire. 'I've already telephoned your mother's assistant and suggested the trip be rearranged for half-term. Rupert said he'd be in touch with you about travel arrangements.'

Adelaide Diamond saw Topaz's face light up. She wasn't happy that Topaz had been invited to go on the trip; last term she'd told her she had to concentrate on her schoolwork and forget about auditions, adverts and becoming a star. But if Topaz had a private invitation to a film set during half-term, there was nothing the school could do about it.

'Thank you, Miss Diamond,' said Sapphire. 'I'm sorry that my mother didn't think about school rules.'

'And as for you, Topaz, you shouldn't have skipped the dance class without permission,' Miss Diamond said stiffly. 'Remember what I told you last term? One more problem and your scholarship will be terminated. Do I make myself clear?'

Topaz nodded. Miss Diamond obviously *didn't* know about the Speedy Snax voice-over or surely she would have mentioned it? She looked closely at Miss Diamond but couldn't see any hint of Noodle-Burger-voice-over-knowledge in her eyes.

'Now off you go,' said the Headmistress. 'Don't keep Mr Feldspar waiting.'

Bob Feldspar, the geography teacher at Precious Gems, was never a particularly happy man, but this term he was even more unhappy than usual.

As a leading light in the Starbridge Strollers amateur dramatics society, Bob Feldspar had shown Adelaide Diamond the programme for their next production. He was secretly hoping that she might offer to come to the opening night of the performance. To get a film star who had won five Golden Nugget awards (even if it was years ago) would be quite something.

'This is wonderful, Bob!' Adelaide had said, flicking through the programme. 'I had no idea you were so talented with computers.'

Bob blushed. 'Just a little hobby of mine,' he said proudly. 'Another string to my bow.'

It was then Adelaide had dropped the bombshell that the IT teacher had finally packed up her super-fast extra-slim laptop and walked out, complaining that the computers at Precious Gems were too old, too slow and too unreliable for someone who prided herself on being at the cutting edge of technology. The school needed someone to teach the first-years IT for one term and Bob Feldspar was the only one who could do it.

'That's such a relief!' Adelaide had said, as she marched away before Bob Feldspar had time to complain or ask her to attend the opening night.

Bob Feldspar wasn't surprised the IT teacher had walked out. The school didn't even have a proper computer suite, just a classroom which doubled as the prop and scenery store. It was like teaching in a forest; last term, the seniors had put on a production of *Babes in the Wood*, and the tree-lined backdrops were still propped against the walls.

As she slumped down in her seat, hidden behind the computer screen, Topaz reflected how unhappy she was that she would be seeing more of Fusty Feldspar. He had never liked her and the incident last term when she had hypnotized Ruby and caused havoc in his lesson was still fresh in her mind.

Bob Feldspar noisily cleared his throat and the class fell silent. 'Something a little different for you today,' he announced. 'We're running a competition in class. I

want you all to design and print a poster for your maypole dancing display at the Starbridge Festival.'

Someone asked whether there would be a prize. Topaz brightened up and popped her head round the computer screen.

Bob Feldspar saw Topaz staring at him and instead of his heart sinking as it usually did when she was in one of his classes, he allowed himself a wry smile at the thought of the easy lesson in front of him. Not even Topaz L'Amour could cause a problem sitting behind a computer, designing a poster.

He began to write on the board the details to go on the poster whilst shouting over his shoulder, 'The prize is that the poster will be used all over Starbridge to advertise your display. Miss Diamond will come in later and judge the winner.'

'Some prize!' Topaz whispered to Ruby who was sitting next to her, peering at the keyboard over the top of her glasses.

Ruby didn't look up. She was already worrying about being in the dance display. She wasn't a dancer – she didn't even take regular dance lessons – but Miss Diamond had suggested she be part of the display as it would help her stage fright, which was still as bad as when she first joined Precious Gems. Nothing had helped, not even performing in assembly or Topaz's attempt at hypnotizing her in the toilets with a swinging ballet shoe. The Director of Music, Gloria Gold, had suggested that Ruby play the music for the dancing display, but even that was too terrifying. In fact, she'd made Miss Gold stand outside the room whilst she played the piano and recorded the music on an old tape recorder. If she couldn't play the piano in front of a teacher, how was she going to dance in front of a crowd of strangers?

Topaz sat in front of the computer screen and typed in the information that Fusty Feldspar had written on the board.

Rhythm in Ribbons – A Display of Dancing
From Pupils at Precious Gems Stage School
(Headmistress: Miss Adelaide Diamond).
Starbridge Festival, Starbridge Common.

She typed the time and the date. She changed the typeface, moved the words around, enlarged some of them, changed the colours and inserted a picture of some dancers. She added a border, made a few final touches and sat back and admired what she had created.

Bob Feldspar noticed Topaz sitting back in her chair, staring at her screen.

That wretched girl is bored already! he thought as he strode over to Topaz, looking forward to telling her off for being lazy. But when he peered over her shoulder, he saw that the poster she had created was by far the best he'd seen all morning. Bob Feldspar couldn't bear to give her any praise so he just grunted, 'Print it out.'

Towards the end of the lesson there was a flurry of activity as the printer whirred into life, jammed and was hit several times on the side with a large book to get it started again. Eventually an assortment of crumpled, torn and chewed posters was laid out on a desk and Miss Diamond swept through the door for the judging.

The class crowded around one side of the desk whilst Miss Diamond stood behind the other. Some of the posters were so terrible there was no way that they could be used, but the Headmistress stood with her grey head bowed as she carefully studied each one for the same amount of time. Eventually she pulled out a poster and held it in the air. 'This is the clear winner!' she said. 'Who did this?'

At the back of the crowd Topaz put up her hand. 'I did, Miss Diamond!' she squealed. 'It's me!'

Even though there was no proper prize, Topaz was surprised to find herself thrilled at being the winner, and too excited to notice Bob Feldspar's pained expression.

'Well done, Topaz,' he said through gritted teeth. 'Sit back down, make sure you have saved the file and we'll arrange to have the poster professionally printed.'

Topaz sat at the keyboard, pressed the 'Save' button and admired her prize-winning work. All those times in Miss Diamond's office, sitting on the lumpy sofa, looking at the old film and theatre posters on the walls had obviously paid off. One day, she wouldn't just be a girl from a tiny top-floor flat in one of the poorer parts of town – one day her name would appear on a poster in a starring role, just as Miss Diamond's had done. She moved the mouse over her poster, drew a star, typed in huge letters: 'Starring Topaz L'Am♥ur!' and giggled. But just as she was about to press the 'Undo' button the screen seemed to suck in her poster and went blank. Topaz stared in horror as the computer burst into life and the screen flashed up the message: 'A Fatal Error Has Occurred.'

Bob Feldspar appeared behind her shoulder. 'I hope you saved your work,' he said in a voice which implied he hoped she hadn't.

Topaz nodded. It wasn't a lie, but it wasn't the whole truth either. She knew she had saved *a* poster; the question was, which one? If the computer had just saved the old version she'd be fine and no one need ever know. But if it was the version with her name on it, she'd be in big trouble. Having won the poster competition there was *no way* she could admit to Fusty Feldspar what she had just done. He already thought she was too big for her dancing shoes, and admitting to adding 'Starring Topaz L'Am♥ur!' would prove it. She'd have to take the chance that everything would be fine.

'You were lucky,' said Bob Feldspar with a curl of his lip. 'I'll retrieve the file and get it printed. See what you can achieve if you concentrate for a change?'

Chapter Four

'It's happened again!' said Topaz, as she put her lunch tray down next to Ruby and Sapphire's. 'I was standing in the queue and I went to say hi to some of the others and they blanked me. Just turned their backs!'

'Can't you think of *anything* you might have done to upset them?' said Ruby, through a mouthful of food. 'I mean, I know we've never been that friendly with the others, but there has to be *something*.'

Topaz shook her head. This had been going on for the last couple of days. Every time she'd seen one of the other first-years they had either ignored her or glared at her. No one had wanted to be her partner in mime class, her toes were deliberately stamped on in tap-dancing and in singing, she was sure that some of the others coughed on purpose when it was her turn to sing a solo.

'I can't think of anything,' she said. 'There's nothing for it but to ask one of them.'

As a pale, thin boy passed by, Topaz grabbed the edge of his blazer and hauled him back. 'Hey, Jasper!' she said. 'Come and eat lunch with us!'

Jasper Pretty glanced nervously at a group of girls on a nearby table. They seemed to be watching him. 'Let go!' he said, trying to pull himself free.

Topaz held firmly on to his blazer. 'Not until you tell me what it is I'm supposed to have done,' she said.

Jasper gave up struggling. 'They say you're a teacher's pet and went behind everyone's backs to secretly work out a different routine for tomorrow's Rhythm in Ribbons display,' he pouted. 'They don't like the fact that you're billed as the star!'

'She's not!' said Sapphire, turning to Topaz. 'Are you?'

Topaz's heart and stomach did a simultaneous flip-flop. The poster! Fusty Feldspar must have retrieved and printed the wrong version – the poster which had her name on. No wonder the others were annoyed. It looked as if *she* was the star! She glanced over at the crowd of girls, who were still staring daggers in her direction.

'Where are these posters?' she asked Jasper. 'I haven't seen them. Who put them up?'

'They're *everywhere*,' he said, giving an almighty tug to pull himself free from Topaz, and sending his lunch spinning off his tray. 'Some of the PTs were given them to put up in return for a free lesson.'

The PTs were the part-time students who came to Precious Gems after their own school for dance and theatre lessons. The full-time students looked down their noses at the PTs, but their fees paid for Topaz's scholarship and, as she had had no stage experience before coming to Precious Gems, she still attended some of the PT classes.

Jasper scurried away, leaving most of his lunch still on the floor.

'It was a mistake,' said Topaz, seeing the questioning expression on her friends' faces. 'I didn't mean to do it. Well, I did, but I didn't mean for anyone to see it! You've got to help me get those posters back! It's not just my name that's the problem. I put my name over the date and time so no one will know about the performance.'

'I don't know what we can do to help,' said Ruby. 'The PTs come from all over town. Those posters will be everywhere!'

Sapphire leant over the table and patted Topaz's arm. 'Topaz, it was a mistake,' she said. 'No one is going to the festival just to see our dance. And once they're at the festival they'll see the maypole anyway.'

Topaz shook her head. 'I've *got* to change those posters. Remember, I've got to be the perfect pupil this term or I'll be packing up my dancing shoes and going to Starbridge High.'

'Miss D isn't going to expel you because of a computer error,' said Sapphire calmly. 'You're worrying over nothing.'

Topaz gave her friends a steely look. 'I can't take that chance,' she said. 'If you won't help me fix those posters, I'll do it myself!'

Ruby and Sapphire looked at each other. Topaz had got it into her head that the posters had to be altered, and *nothing* was going to change her mind.

'OK,' said Ruby, 'we'll help you. But I don't see how we are going to get them all changed in time. We'd be walking around Starbridge for days.'

'There is a way of getting all those posters changed quickly,' said Sapphire.

'How?' asked Topaz and Ruby in unison.

Sapphire gave a mischievous smile. 'You're forgetting I have a chauffeur-driven car at my disposal.'

Topaz spent the evening making hundreds of large

paper stars on which she wrote: 'Today! 11 a.m. and 2 p.m.' Her hands ached from cutting out the points on the stars and it was the early hours of the morning before she climbed into bed, only for the alarm to go off a few hours later.

It's my own fault, she thought as she splashed cold water on her face. *If only I'd owned up to my mistake in the first place, none of this would have happened.*

She grabbed her bag, pulled on the Precious Gems T-shirt with the school motto, 'We Sparkle Whatever the Occasion' across the back, wriggled into a black skirt with coloured ribbons round the hem, found her dancing shoes, and stumbled down the stairs into the waiting car.

Parks the chauffeur didn't seem the slightest bit surprised that Vanessa Stratton's daughter had asked him to get up early and spend Saturday morning driving her and her friends around Starbridge to find posters. He was used to the strange demands of film stars and their families. Once he had driven hundreds of miles for a packet of mints, because no one could find Vanessa Stratton's favourite brand in the shops near to where she was filming.

There was no sign of Ruby as Parks pulled into Stellar Terrace and stopped outside Precious Gems. Sapphire and Topaz got out of the car and walked round to the East Wing where Ruby was a weekly boarder, the journey back to her home in Sutton Perry being too long to do each day.

'She must have slept in by mistake,' said Topaz as they looked up at the darkened windows. 'She wouldn't let us down otherwise.'

They called her name, went back to ask Parks to toot the horn, but there was still no sign of Ruby.

'Let's knock on the window,' said Topaz, bending down to pick up a few tiny stones. She threw them at the window, but missed, and they clattered down the wall. There was still no sign of life. She tried again and this time managed to hit the window. They waited for a light to click on and the window to open, but the room remained dark.

'She's not hearing us. I need something bigger,' said Topaz, looking around.

'Not too big!' said Sapphire – too late – as Topaz lobbed a large pebble towards the window, just as Ruby opened it. The stone hit the left lens of Ruby's glasses, sending a huge crack through the centre.

'Yeow!' she yelled, staggering backwards.

'At least I only broke a little piece of glass,' said Topaz, looking at Sapphire's face. 'It was better than breaking a whole window.'

Ruby ran down the stairs and slumped into the back

seat of the car. 'Look at my glasses!' she said. 'I can hardly see!'

'Sorry, Rubes,' said Topaz. 'We thought you'd overslept.'

'I did,' said Ruby. 'But I didn't expect a rock in my eye as an alarm clock.'

Even with a chauffeur who knew every inch of Starbridge, finding the posters took hours. The PTs had done a very good job. There were posters on trees, telephone boxes, notice-boards, lampposts and bus shelters. There was even a poster outside Starbridge High. Topaz shuddered at the thought that Kylie Slate and her gang might have seen her name on the poster and wondered whether she might see them at the festival later that day. Every school in Starbridge was supposed to provide some form of entertainment, but there was no way that Kylie and her gang would do anything other than come and jeer at the others.

Topaz looked at her watch. 'We're going to be late *and* we've missed the rehearsal!' she said. 'Anton Graphite will be furious!'

Parks turned round in his seat and said, 'Miss Stratton, shall we call it a day?'

'Yes thank you, Parks,' replied Sapphire, as Parks accelerated towards Starbridge Common. 'We'll leave our bags in the car and pick them up later.'

'I don't think I can see to dance,' said Ruby. '*And* I feel dizzy!'

'You'll be fine,' said Topaz. 'It's only follow-the-leader, but with ribbons. You're dancing behind me, so just follow me. What can possibly go wrong?'

Chapter Five

It was a bright day with just a light, warm breeze and crowds of people were already streaming over Starbridge Common.

'Don't go so fast,' gasped Ruby, lagging behind as they hurried past the bouncy castle, tombola stalls, face-painting and coconut shies. 'Everything looks blurry.'

'You'll be fine,' Topaz shouted back over her shoulder as they headed towards the soaring maypole, its coloured ribbons fluttering in the breeze.

The Precious Gems dance choreographer, Anton Graphite, glared at Topaz as she emerged through the crowd. As if it wasn't bad enough choreographing first-years dancing around a maypole, he had first-years who hadn't even bothered to turn up for the rehearsal. There were *so* many other things he'd rather be doing on a Saturday.

'Grab your ribbons,' he instructed in a clipped voice. 'Gloria?'

He nodded towards pipe-cleaner-thin Gloria Gold, who was bent over an old tape recorder, her long bony finger hovering over the 'On' button. Gloria didn't mind giving up her Saturday to help Anton. There was nowhere else she'd rather be.

Anton puffed out his chest and announced to the waiting crowd, 'Precious Gems Stage School invites you to watch Rhythm in Ribbons – a display of music and dance!'

He nodded again at Gloria who hit the 'On' button, and with an almighty clunk, the tape recorder burst into life, belting out the piano music Ruby had recorded.

People peered over shoulders and through gaps in the crowd to catch a glimpse of pupils who might, one day, be famous stars. Topaz danced in front of Ruby and behind Sapphire, her friend's blonde hair swinging in time to the music as they weaved in and out of the ribbons.

As Topaz did another circuit of the maypole, she saw Kylie Slate and Janice Stone elbow their way to the front of the crowd. Kylie was wearing a pair of tracksuit bottoms rolled *way* too low down past her hips and a tiny vest top that was *far* too tight. She was blowing huge pink bubble-gum bubbles which she popped with a snap every time Topaz danced past.

'Ooh, if it isn't little Miss Famous Twinkle-toes!' Kylie shouted over the music.

I'm just going to ignore her, Topaz thought to herself. *She's not going to spoil the performance.*

Eventually, it was time for the grand finale – the reverse double twist and spin. Anton Graphite had been designing the dance for weeks and was very proud of it. It required speed and concentration as ribbons were quickly passed from dancer to dancer to form what looked like a tightly woven straw hat.

Even though Kylie and Janice were still watching (and Kylie was still sneering and blowing gum bubbles), Topaz was enjoying herself skipping under and over the ribbons, counting the steps around the maypole. Out of the corner of her eye, she saw Kylie waving her arms and pointing.

I'm not even going to look in their direction, thought Topaz, putting her nose in the air and spinning round the maypole. *They're not worth it.*

'Watch Carrot Top!' Kylie yelled as Topaz spun round again.

Topaz danced on, determined to ignore Kylie's shouting.

'Don't forget Four-eyes!' Kylie yelled again.

It was no good. Topaz might be able to ignore Kylie but she couldn't let her bully Ruby.

'Ignore them, Ruby,' she called back over her shoulder. 'Kylie's a cow!'

Suddenly, Janice shouted out, 'Topaz! The girl with the plaits!'

Something must *be wrong*, thought Topaz. Janice might now be Kylie's best friend rather than hers, but she wouldn't taunt Ruby.

She looked back over her shoulder, but instead of Ruby dancing behind her, Jasper Pretty was following, his eyes fixed wide with horror.

'Where's Ruby?' mouthed Topaz, trying to smile, dance, watch where she was going *and* look back over her shoulder at the same time.

Before Jasper could mouth back a reply, she saw her friend. Somehow, Ruby's plaits had got caught up in the ribbons and with every turn around the maypole, Ruby was getting closer and closer to the centre pole. Anton Graphite hadn't noticed. He was smiling smugly to himself and watching the audience enjoy the dance he had created. Gloria Gold was watching Anton and thinking how clever he was to choreograph such a complicated dance.

I've got to do something, thought Topaz, as Ruby became tied tighter and tighter to the maypole.

Dropping her ribbon, she rushed
over to the tape recorder, pushed
Gloria Gold out of the way and hit
the 'Off' button. There were yells
and shrieks as the dancers crashed
into one another and fell over;
some stopped and others tried to
carry on dancing. Anton Graphite
turned purple with rage and Gloria
Gold looked as if she might faint.
Ruby stood pinned to the maypole,
looking like an Egyptian mummy, her
broken glasses poking out from behind a bandage of
candy-coloured ribbons.

Try as they might, they were unable to unwind
her. Eventually someone found a pair of scissors
and carefully, and amidst cries of 'Mind her plaits!'
and 'Don't cut her fingers!', Ruby eventually stumbled
free from her chains of ribbons and burst into
tears.

'What happened?' asked Topaz. 'How did it all go so
wrong?'

Ruby took off her shattered glasses. 'I couldn't see
properly and I felt so dizzy I just got slower and slower,
and then someone grabbed my plaits instead of a
ribbon and then I just seemed to get passed around the
maypole by my plaits and then I got wound round the

pole and . . .' Ruby burst into floods of tears again. 'I just want to go home.'

'Let's get you back to Precious Gems,' said Sapphire, putting her arm around Ruby.

'No, I want to go home,' sobbed Ruby. 'I want to go to Sutton Perry and get my spare glasses. I can't do another performance.'

The girls looked at the maypole. There wasn't going to be another performance. In trying to free Ruby the ribbons had been cut to shreds and now the maypole looked as if it had been given a very bad and brutal haircut.

'We'll find Parks,' said Sapphire, leading Ruby away. 'He'll run you home. Everything will be OK. I promise.'

Topaz felt wretched. This was *all* her fault. If she had told the truth about the poster from the start none of this would have happened. Now the maypole was ruined, there wouldn't be another performance, Anton Graphite was furious and Miss Diamond was bound to ask Ruby what had happened. Changing her poster at the last minute hadn't just been a disaster. It was a disaster with catastrophic consequences. A major disastrophe. She never meant to get her friends in trouble – she wanted to be a good friend, but somehow she always managed to drag them into her problems.

47

On Topaz's three-level disaster scale, this was *definitely* a disastrophe. The 3D-scale started with disasterettes, which were just minor annoyances, then progressed to disasters and finally disastrophes, which were the worst possible disasters in the worst possible context with catastrophic consequences for life.

Take a cold. An ordinary run-of-the-mill sort of cold which gave you a red nose, watery eyes and sudden sneezes. To get a cold that made you feel grotty was always a disasterette, unless, of course, you were supposed to have revised for a test but hadn't done *any* revision. Then you could pretend to your mum that you felt so *terrible* you couldn't *possibly* go to school, so that whilst everyone else was sweating over equations, you could be at home lying on the sofa, reading magazines. If, on the other hand, you had a cold on the morning of an audition with a top casting director, a disasterette escalated into a disaster. If you didn't go to the audition you were losing a chance of stardom, but if you *did* go the director wouldn't see you at your starring best. There was nothing for it but to go and hope that the casting director would look at you and think to himself, *Behind the runny nose and red eyes, that girl is a star!* and pull you out of the line-up.

But suppose you had managed to avert the disaster of being passed over because of a cold, the casting director *had* pulled you out of the line-up and was now asking you your name. Instead of saying, 'My name is Topaz L'Amour!' and smiling brightly at the director, your nose was so bunged up with cold all you could manage to mutter was 'By bame ib Bobaz B'Amour', before sneezing loudly and spraying snot all over the casting director. You didn't get the part, obviously, but worse, the director caught your cold, which then turned into bronchitis and pneumonia, leaving him ill for weeks and vowing *never* to give you a part! *That* was a full-scale disastrophe.

If Miss D asks what went wrong I'll own up, thought Topaz, looking at the wrecked maypole. *I won't let Ruby get into trouble just because of me, even if it means I lose my scholarship and have to leave stage school.*

Topaz began to wander aimlessly through the crowds. She saw Octavia Quaver's friend, Melody Sharp, standing outside a tent with a sign saying, 'Madame Catovia – Fortune-Teller – Cross My Palm With Silver and I Will Predict Your Future.'

If only she could, thought Topaz. *She could tell me whether Miss D is going to find out about the Speedy Snax advert, if I'm going to lose my scholarship and whether I'm going to become a star!*

She saw Kylie Slate swing round the corner. It had been bad enough her jeering during the performance.

Topaz couldn't face seeing her on her own. She turned to walk quickly in the other direction, only to see a stony-faced Anton Graphite come into view.

I've got to hide! she thought, diving into the fortune-teller's tent and peering through the gaps in the beaded curtain as she waited for Kylie and Anton to go past.

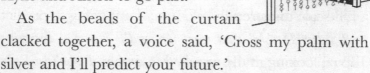

As the beads of the curtain clacked together, a voice said, 'Cross my palm with silver and I'll predict your future.'

Topaz realized that she didn't have any money on her, not even her bus pass. She'd left her bag in the back of Sapphire's car, which was now on its way to Sutton Perry with Ruby. It would be a long walk back to Andromeda Road in her dancing-shoes and ribboned skirt.

'I'm just hiding in here,' she said, still peering anxiously through the curtain. 'I don't have any money on me.'

'Then I will predict your future for free!' said the voice.

Topaz turned round and a saw a small woman sitting behind a table. She was hunched over a crystal ball, rubbing it with her hands in their white lace gloves.

Huge gold earrings dangled from beneath a scarf wrapped round her head and a veil covered her face, except for her eyes which were cast down, staring at the crystal ball.

Even though Topaz knew it was probably just one of the teachers from another school dressed up to look like a fortune-teller, the woman had a menacing air about her.

'No, honestly,' said Topaz. 'I'm just hiding in here, really.'

'Sit!' commanded the woman. 'I am going to predict your future.'

Oh well, thought Topaz. *I could do with a laugh.*

Topaz sat in front of the woman who kept her head down, peering into the crystal ball.

'I am the daughter of the great Madame Lupina and I know *everything*!' said the woman. 'I know that you want to be a star!'

Topaz sat up straight with shock.

The woman continued to rub the crystal ball. 'The ball tells me you are trying *everything* to become a star. You even hoped your voice would make you a star!'

Topaz's eyes widened. The Speedy Snax voice-over! How could Madame Catovia know about that? She'd only told Sapphire and Ruby. Even her mum didn't know.

The woman stared into the crystal ball. 'You want to be a star. You want to ride in big cars and sign your autograph for fans.'

Topaz began to feel uneasy. Madame Catovia seemed to know a great deal about her. Was it possible she *could* see into the future after all?

Topaz leant forward and peered into the crystal ball, but she couldn't see anything other than her own distorted reflection.

'Will I be a star?' she asked anxiously. 'Will I be famous?'

The woman shook her bowed head. 'You don't have what it takes,' she said.

'That's not true!' cried Topaz. 'How can you say that?'

Madame Catovia hunched further over the ball. 'The ball tells all! The ball *never* lies,' she said. 'It tells me you will *never* be a star. You will be forever taking one step forward and two steps back.'

'Why?' asked Topaz indignantly.

The fortune-teller seemed irritated. 'Because you have no talent and your acting is pants!' she flashed. 'Now go!'

What a weird thing for fortune-teller to say! thought Topaz.

As she was about to leave the tent, Topaz turned, and for a split-second, saw Madame Catovia staring at her with hard, glittering eyes – eyes that made Topaz feel uneasy and sent a chill down her spine.

Silly old woman, she thought. *Of course I'm going to be a star.*

As Topaz stepped out of the tent she looked up. The bright day had vanished and the sky was inky black. There was a flash of lightning, a clap of thunder and rain began to pour down. The common was already nearly empty as people rushed for shelter.

'Nice skirt, saddo!' sneered Kylie as she ran past, arm in arm with Janice Stone.

Topaz began to trudge home in the pouring rain. Her thick black skirt seemed to soak up every raindrop and her dance-shoes were meant for dancing, not wading through puddles.

As a bus went past and sprayed dirty water up her skirt, Topaz saw Kylie Slate spit her bubble-gum out of the window, but before Topaz could step out of the way, she had trodden on it. She tried to take a step forward but the bubble-gum stuck her shoe to the pavement. She then tried to scrape it off by walking backwards but still the gum wouldn't move. As the rain lashed down, she remembered one of Madame Catovia's predictions. 'You will never be a star. You will be forever taking one step forward and two steps back.'

Topaz thought of Madame Catovia's evil eyes and

shuddered. 'Just a coincidence,' she said to herself, trying to believe it.

Chapter Six

'When I get my passport, does it have to have my real name on it or can I use my stage name?' Topaz asked her mother over breakfast one morning. She'd changed her name from Love to L'Amour when she'd started at stage school because she thought L'Amour sounded much more glamorous, but she'd never owned up to Ruby and Sapphire that L'Amour wasn't her real name. The passport might give the game away.

'I'm not happy about this trip to Palm Island,' said Lola Love. 'Sapphire's mother hasn't rung me to talk to me about the arrangements and it's half-term soon.'

'Mum!' Topaz said in an exasperated voice. 'Of *course* Mrs Stratton wouldn't phone you. She doesn't phone anyone! Her assistant, Rupert, will do it.'

Lola began to clear away the mugs and plates. 'Well, whoever was supposed to call me, no one has,' she said. 'I'd really like to know what's going on.'

So would I, thought Topaz to herself, and said, 'I'll ask Sapphire later.'

'I don't even know if we can afford for you to go,' said Lola.

'Afford what?' said Topaz defiantly. 'It's all expenses paid!'

'You'll still need some new clothes and some spending money,' said Lola.

'You've never wanted me to be a star,' Topaz sulked. 'You're always trying to stop me.'

Lola Love looked at her daughter. 'That's not fair, Topaz, and you know it.' She sounded angry.

'You don't like me mixing with show business people, do you?' persisted Topaz. 'But you never tell me why!'

Lola put on her coat and picked up her bag. One day she would tell her daughter about the time she had been in show business; how *she* had dreamt of becoming a star, and how it had all gone wrong.

'This isn't about me stopping your dreams,' Lola said, heading for the door. 'Money's especially tight right now. I might have to fit in another job. Maybe I could get a few hours on the checkout at the Bargain Basket supermarket.'

* * *

Topaz stood at the bus stop and thought about her mother. She felt guilty about being so horrible to her sometimes. Lola Love did her best for both of them. She cleaned offices early in the morning before the workers arrived, tried to get back to see Topaz off to school and then cleaned private houses during the day. Then after making Topaz her tea, she'd leave again to clean more offices late at night.

Topaz's scholarship paid for her school fees but not her uniform, and stage school uniform was *very* expensive. It wasn't just the usual blazer, skirt and PE kit, but also tap shoes and ballet shoes, leotards and skirts, and all sorts of other things that people at ordinary schools never thought of. No wonder money was tight.

Sapphire's mum was glamorous and exciting, but Topaz wasn't sure she was a very nice person. Sapphire never seemed to have anything good to say about her. And Ruby hardly ever mentioned *her* mum. Topaz thought of her own mum and smiled. She was definitely the best!

Topaz wondered how she could help. There was a bit of money in her savings account from the Zit Stop! advert she'd done, but her agent Zelma Flint hadn't paid her as much as she had expected.

Zelma Flint! thought Topaz. In worrying about Miss Diamond finding out about the Speedy Snax advert, she'd completely forgotten she'd hadn't received any money for the voice-over. That was bound to pay for a new swimsuit and a pair of flip-flops, but she'd have to confess to her mum about the voice-over or she would wonder how Topaz had suddenly come into money. It was time to ring Zelma.

From the day Topaz had met Zelma Flint in Miss Diamond's office and Zelma had handed Topaz her business card saying, 'I could make you a star,' Topaz had been carrying that card round in her purse. She fished it out and pulled her mobile phone from her bag. Her mum had made her promise to use it only in emergencies, but surely not being paid by your agent counted as an emergency?

She dialled the number.

A high-pitched voice answered. 'Zelma Flint's office. This is Jack speaking. How may I help you?'

'Could I speak to Zelma Flint, please?' asked Topaz.

'Let's see,' said Jack. There was a rustling of papers at the other end of the phone. 'Miss Flint is a *very* busy woman. She has a conference call at nine, a meeting at nine-fifteen, another call at nine—'

'I just want to speak to her,' said Topaz. 'My name is Topaz L'Amour.'

The rustling of papers stopped and Jack shrieked,

'Topaz! Why didn't you say! I'll put you straight through.'

Before Zelma Flint even spoke, Topaz could tell by the rasping sound of her breath she was on the line. 'Topaz!' she wheezed. 'How lovely to hear from you. What can I do for you?'

Topaz gulped and said, 'I don't seem to have been paid for the Speedy Snax voice-over.'

'Haven't you?' said Zelma, taking a drag on her cigarette. 'You should have been. Let me get Jack to pull the file. Hang on a moment.'

There was a click, a pause, another click and Zelma came back on the line. 'It seems, honey, that we are in what is known in the industry as an even-stevens situation.'

'Which means?' asked Topaz.

'There's no money,' said Zelma.

'No money!' gasped Topaz. 'How come?'

At the other end of the phone, Zelma swung her feet on to her desk and flicked cigarette ash off her skirt. 'You see, Topaz, this was the first proper job you did directly with me. There were set-up costs which came off your fee.'

'Set-up costs?' queried Topaz. 'What set-up costs?'

'There was a signing-on fee, then the usual fee I take for each job, a fee for drawing up the contract, a fee for your publicity photographs, the fee for . . .'

'But I haven't got a contract with you!' said Topaz. 'I haven't had any publicity photographs taken! I got paid for the Zit Stop! advert. Why not this one?'

'You'll start earning money from your next job,' said Zelma. 'Must fly. Bye!'

The line clicked and Topaz was left listening to the dialling tone.

I've been double crossed! she thought as she stuck out her arm to get the approaching bus to stop. *Now what do I do?*

'Still no word from your mum?' said Topaz as she, Sapphire and Ruby sat in Happy Al's Café after school, drinking hot chocolates and sharing one cheese toastie between the three of them.

'Not yet,' said Sapphire. 'But you know my mum's a very last-minute sort of person.'

'Mine isn't,' said Ruby. 'She's already getting herself into a state over whether I've got the right clothes and if she'll get all the ironing done in time.'

'You won't need much,' said Sapphire. 'Just something comfortable to travel in; a couple of nice dresses for the other end as there are bound to be some parties to go to; stuff for the beach; ordinary clothes . . .'

'Sounds expensive,' said Topaz glumly, shocked at how like her mother she sounded. 'I rang Zelma Flint about my Noodle Burger money but she says she doesn't owe me any. She says everything I've earned so far she needs to take in set-up fees.'

Behind the counter, the mention of Zelma Flint's name caused Happy Al to stop polishing his new state-of-the-art chrome Turbo Frother cappuccino machine, complete with multi-directional froth nozzle and turbo steam jet. So far, he hadn't been able to bring himself actually to make coffee with it as he couldn't bear to get it dirty, but he enjoyed polishing the chrome and hearing steam whoosh through the pipes. If it hadn't been for Topaz mentioning his café when she had won the game show, *Proof of the Pudding* – sending customers flooding through the door to try his chocolate mousse – he might never have been able to afford the Turbo Frother.

'Zelma Flint?' barked Al from behind the counter. 'Don't go anywhere near that woman.'

'I already have,' said Topaz. 'She's my agent, sort of.'

Al thought back to the days when Zelma was *his* agent. The days when he played Inspector Barry 'Nosey' Parker in the prime-time TV series *Murder Mile*. He'd been a big star with people stopping him in the street, asking for his autograph. He'd had his own table at Starbridge's top restaurant, The Truffle Pig, and pretty girls always at his side, much to the annoyance of his then wife, Norma. In those days, Zelma Flint was never off the phone, ringing him to invite him to a film première, the opening of a new nightclub or arranging interviews with celebrity magazines. But when *Murder Mile* was moved from its prime-time Saturday night slot to last thing at night on Monday, ratings plummeted until eventually *International Speed Tiddlywinks*, shown on another channel, was getting twice the viewing figures of *Murder Mile*. Zelma stopped calling. When Pulsar Television finally cancelled the series, Zelma not only stopped calling, she stopped taking Al's calls.

He picked up a tea towel and angrily flicked the counter. 'Stay clear of that woman,' he said. 'She's a slimy, two-faced, double-crossing untrustworthy good-for-nothing waste of space. If she walked in here tomorrow and offered me a part I wouldn't think twice about turning it down.'

'So you don't like her, then,' said Topaz.

'Like her?' Al snapped. '*Nothing* would persuade me to work for Zelma Flint ever again.'

'So what are you going to do about Zelma?' asked Sapphire as Al went back to polishing the Turbo Frother.

'I'll think of something,' said Topaz, without the faintest idea what she was going to do next. 'When do you think your mum might be in touch?'

Sapphire shrugged. 'I'll ring Rupert now and try and find out what's going on.' She pulled a shiny silver mobile phone out of her bag, flipped open the cover and pressed the speed dial. 'Rupert?' she asked. 'This is Sapphire. Is my mother there?'

Topaz and Ruby could hear Rupert's shrill voice crackling through the phone.

'Since when?' demanded Sapphire.

There was more agitated high-pitched crackle. Topaz could tell there was a problem.

'Rupert, you know full well that she promised me and my friends a trip to the set.' Sapphire sounded calm but firm. 'We were promised parts in the movie.'

It seemed that despite Vanessa's grand gesture, the chance to be in her film had fallen through. Sapphire always said her mother was unreliable, and she was right.

'Rupert,' said Sapphire with an unusually icy tone, 'my mother promised me and my friends a visit to the set. I don't care where she is or what excuses she gives, I want her to keep that promise!' She snapped shut the case of her mobile phone and tossed it on the table.

'It seems,' she said rolling her eyes, 'that my mother finished filming a week ago and is now cruising to somewhere hot on a yacht. No one thought to tell me.'

Topaz tried not to let her disappointment show. After all, the only reason they were going to the film set in the first place was so that Sapphire could spend time with her mother. It must be even more disappointing for her. But Sapphire wasn't disappointed. She was furious.

'It's OK,' said Topaz. 'It's not your fault. You know what mothers can be like!'

'She made a promise,' said Sapphire angrily, 'and I'm going to make sure she keeps it! Rupert's going to ring back.'

Topaz, Sapphire and Ruby all watched the mobile phone for what seemed like an eternity, until finally it rang and Sapphire answered it.

'Yes, Rupert, I see,' she said. 'Thanks for letting me know.'

'There's good news and bad news,' she announced after she had finished talking to Rupert.

'The good news?' asked Ruby.

'The good news is that when the director saw the end of the film in editing he didn't like the final scene where Sister Ursula and Father O'Leary leave the orphans at the airport. He wants to re-shoot it with more orphans. We all have parts as extras in the film. The scene is being shot during half-term.'

Topaz nearly fell off her seat with delight. 'When are

the plane tickets arriving?' she said, trying not to think about how she was going to be able to afford it.

'There won't be any,' said Sapphire.

Topaz looked worried. Vanessa had promised them the use of a private plane. Did this mean they had to buy their own tickets? Her mum might be able to stretch to buying a new pair of jeans and a top, but not aeroplane tickets.

Sapphire saw the disappointed look on her friends' faces. 'That's the bad news. There's no trip to Palm Island. The extra scene is being filmed in the car park of the Starbridge branch of The Bargain Basket.'

Chapter Seven

Topaz spent the days of half-term before filming wandering around the flat dreaming, practising her autograph, smiling at imaginary photographers and waving graciously at pretend crowds of adoring fans. Although she'd been disappointed not to go somewhere exotic to film the scene, it was still exciting to be in a film – *any* film – and it did solve the problem of needing an expensive new wardrobe and a passport. There was still the possibility that from out of the crowd of extras, she would be noticed; that somehow, somewhere, a top director or casting agent would notice the way she played her part and say, 'Who *is* that girl? She's amazing! Pull her out of the crowd and make her a star!'

Topaz waited outside the Andromeda Road flats very early on Wednesday morning for Parks to pick her up. It occurred to her that although it had taken two terms for Sapphire to admit that she had the use of a chauffeur and was driven to school every day, Topaz now hopped in and out of the car in the same way that she used the bus. The Bargain Basket car park was only a ten-minute walk from the flat, but it seemed only natural that if you were going to a film set, you should be driven there.

She waved as Parks pulled up alongside her and jumped in the back next to Ruby and Sapphire. The car pulled away and out into the traffic, stopping outside The Bargain Basket just moments later.

A long queue of people snaked around the outskirts of the car park.

'Who are all these people?' asked Topaz as they joined the end of the queue. 'Do they get paid?'

'Film extras,' said Sapphire. 'They just come to make up the numbers in crowd scenes, street scenes and so on.'

They shuffled forward in the queue until eventually they reached the front where a row of girls dressed in T-shirts emblazoned with the Magnicolour Films logo sat behind trestle tables, handing out forms and pens. *Name; Address; Age; Telephone.* Topaz looked at the space which said *Agent/Agency.*

I'm never *working with Zelma Flint ever again!* she thought, leaving the space blank.

Topaz noticed a small, scruffy-looking man crouched on a box beside a row of Bargain Basket supermarket trolleys. He had a grey beard, glasses and was wearing a creased denim shirt and a battered baseball cap. Topaz didn't like the way he seemed to be looking everyone up and down as they were waved through the line of trestle tables and into the car park.

'You'd think they'd move that scruffy man on,' said Topaz. 'I'm surprised that someone hasn't called security.'

'What man?' asked Ruby.

'The beardy-weirdy,' said Topaz, pointing at the man. 'Over there.'

Sapphire looked over her shoulder. 'That's no beardy-weirdy,' she said. 'That's the director, Joshua P. Finkleberg.'

Topaz groaned and hoped that Joshua P. Finkleberg, director of some of the greatest movies of all time, hadn't heard her call him a beardy-weirdy.

An anxious little man approached and bobbed his

head at Sapphire. 'Miss Sapphire Stratton?' he enquired in a light, clipped voice.

Sapphire nodded.

'I'm such a fan of your mother's,' he gushed. 'I'm from the publicity department at Magnicolour Films. My name's Quentin and I'm *thrilled* to meet you.' The man clasped his hands together in excitement as if he had longed to meet Sapphire all his life. '*Your* people spoke to *our* people who told *me* to tell *you* that you are to be escorted right to the front of the action!' Quentin clapped his hands and looked like an over-excited seal waving its flippers at the thought of a mouthful of fish. 'Isn't that *marvellous*?'

Ruby didn't think so. She hadn't wanted to be right at the front of the action. She wanted to blend into the crowd, especially as she was still wearing her spare pair of glasses, which were hideous. The thought of a camera being anywhere near made her insides churn with nerves.

Topaz was practically dancing on the spot with excitement. *The front of the crowd!* she thought, as they followed Quentin through the car park, past all the other extras who seemed to be aimlessly milling about, waiting for instructions. *This is what it's like to get star treatment!*

Quentin led them to an area which looked like a giant cattle pen.

'The scene will be shot from in front of here,' he said, pointing at a camera on the other side of one of the barriers. 'The rest of the crowd will be let through soon. Make sure you don't get pushed to the back, and if you do, just tell them the guys in publicity *demanded* that the Stratton party be given special treatment!' Quentin beamed and scuttled off.

Ruby's insides were still churning with nerves. 'I'm off to find a toilet,' she said, heading out of the cattle pen.

Topaz looked around her. The car park of The Bargain Basket didn't look anything like an airport runway. There were still shopping trolleys dotted about, a Bargain Basket lorry parked to one side, and a couple of cars which could have been abandoned, or perhaps the owners had somehow become locked in the supermarket overnight and couldn't get out to claim them. As well as the camera opposite, a camera crane hovered overhead, and enormous lights, dimmed but ready to burst into life, hung from scaffolding. Vanessa Stratton may not have flown them by private jet to Palm Island, but at least she had arranged for them to be in the thick of the action.

'This is brilliant!' said Topaz, already imagining herself on screen. 'You will thank your mum for organizing it, won't you?'

Sapphire shrugged. 'I doubt she even knows we're here,' she said. 'I bet Rupert arranged it.'

Around and behind them the car park began to fill up. This was going to be a very big crowd scene and Topaz wondered if the car park was going to be large enough to hold so many orphans.

'I've just seen a girl who looks exactly like Octavia Quaver,' said Ruby, back from her visit to the row of portable loos.

Topaz spun her head round to look at Ruby and gasped, 'Not . . . the Evil One?'

Ruby nodded. 'Don't worry, when I looked again it wasn't her. This girl looked dreadful and Octavia always looks so neat.'

Topaz breathed a sigh of relief. She hadn't seen Octavia since she'd opened the limo door at Starbridge Airport and sent Octavia, her sombrero and her straw donkey spinning on to the pavement. The last thing she needed was for Octavia to start whining about how she'd lost the swimwear catalogue modelling job.

The crane was lowered to the ground and Joshua P. Finkleberg and a camera man got on board before it soared high into the sky, hovering over the crowd, occasionally swooping down over their heads. Topaz practised her best smile for when the camera zoomed in again.

Suddenly, she felt a sharp elbow in her back and a push in her side.

'Move!' a shrill voice ordered. 'You're standing in *my* spot.'

Topaz swung round to come face to face with Octavia Quaver. But something *terrible* had obviously happened to Octavia. She looked *dreadful*. Her usual bouncy blonde curls were dark with grease. Her face seemed to be covered in streaky fake-tan and her clothes, although clean, were old and shabby. The Quaver family had obviously landed on hard times. Perhaps the Quavers had badly needed the money and Octavia *had* lost the modelling job for Fin and Flipper swimwear. For a fleeting moment, Topaz felt a stab of pity for Octavia. Not for long.

'I said, you're standing in *my* spot!' Octavia snarled again.

'This is *our* place!' Topaz snapped back. 'If you don't believe me, just ask Sapphire.'

Sapphire didn't particularly want to be at the front of the crowd, but she wasn't going to be bossed around by Octavia Quaver.

'Quentin from PR told us to stand here,' she said. 'This is *our* spot.'

'I think you'll find that this is *my* spot!' Octavia replied, curling her top lip. 'Ask Quentin yourself!'

Quentin appeared in front of the barrier, clasping his hands. 'Everything all right, ladies?' he asked.

Sapphire gave him a brittle smile. 'Actually, Quentin, it isn't,' she said. 'My friends and I were led to believe we would be standing here, directly in front of the camera. We seem to have lost our place to someone else.' She nodded in the direction of Octavia who stood stony-faced, her hands folded across her chest.

Quentin gave a nervous little cough and lowered his eyes. 'Mr Finkleberg himself picked Miss Quaver out of the crowd to play one of the orphans waving the happy couple goodbye. Miss Quaver will be playing Girl With Hanky.'

Sapphire glared at Quentin who continued to look embarrassed.

Topaz glared at Octavia who looked smug. 'Why couldn't one of us play Girl With Hanky?' she asked Quentin. 'Why her?'

Quentin looked at Topaz, wrinkled his nose slightly and said, 'Mr Finkleberg obviously felt you weren't right for the part.'

Octavia sniggered.

'Well, Quentin,' said Sapphire coolly. '*My* people will definitely be having a word with *your* people when all this is over!'

Quentin flounced off and everyone stood in stony silence.

Topaz couldn't understand what it was about Octavia that had caused Mr Finkleberg to pull her out of the crowd instead of someone else, especially as Octavia looked so dreadful!

Perhaps Mr Finkleberg did hear me, after all, thought Topaz, glancing sideways at Octavia.

As if reading her mind, Octavia snorted, 'You had *no* chance of being picked as Hanky Girl dressed like that! The camera was *never* going to zoom in on you.'

Topaz looked down at her jeans and blue sweatshirt. She'd thought she looked rather good when she'd left the house that morning, certainly better than a greasy-haired, brown-faced, badly-dressed Octavia.

'And you think *you* look good?' Topaz snapped back. 'I suppose it's better than being dressed as a giant burger with a slice of tomato for a hat!'

'I look the part!' retorted Octavia. 'Mum rang the film company, found out all about the film, where and when it was supposed to have been set. *I'm* dressed as a penniless orphan living in a poor sun-drenched country. *You're* dressed like every other girl from Starbridge! Face it. *You* don't have what it takes to be a star. *You* just don't have it in you!'

Topaz realized that Octavia was right. They might both want to be stars, but Octavia actually seemed to know how to go about it. She shuddered as she remembered Madame Catovia saying the same thing.

'I didn't think . . .' began Topaz.

Octavia sneered. 'Of course not! You Precious Gems girls never do!'

Topaz couldn't think of anything to say except, 'Is Melody Sharp here?'

Octavia shrugged. 'She's around somewhere, I suppose. I left her at the back of the queue, holding my clothes. You don't think I came looking like this, do you?'

Topaz was tempted to tell Octavia that *she'd* come in Vanessa Stratton's chauffeur-driven car, but it seemed pointless. Octavia was going to be Hanky Girl and Topaz was just a face in the crowd.

'One, two! One, two!' a voice boomed over a loud hailer.

Huge arc lights suddenly burst into life, so that the atmosphere felt more like a summer's day on a beach than a slightly grey day in a supermarket car park. The crane hovered over the crowd like a vulture waiting to swoop down and grab its prey, or in this case, the perfect shot.

The loud hailer crackled again as Joshua P. Finkleberg barked his instructions: 'Immerse yourself in the scene. The happy couple are leaving the orphanage for the last time. They're flying off to a new life. You're still here. You're happy for them. Gutted for yourselves. I want emotion. I want rivers of tears. *Torrents* of tears! Think about your pet dog dying, if it helps. Lots of waving but no hanky waving unless you are the designated Hanky Girl.'

Octavia gave a little wave of her hanky to show everyone that she was the designated Hanky Girl.

'OK! Relax, everybody. Ready to roll and . . . ACTION!'

The crowd in the Bargain Basket car park waved and cried as if they really were standing on a hot dusty runway, seeing their beloved Sister Ursula and Father O'Leary for the last time. The crane slowly dived and swooped above them, at one point zooming in towards Octavia who was crying and waving her hanky as if her life depended on it.

As the camera closed in, Ruby buried her head in her hands. *There's no way I am going to appear in this film*, she thought to herself.

Sapphire was surprised to find that the thought of her mother leaving an airport – even if dressed as a nun and about to marry a priest – brought tears to her eyes. *I do miss not having her around*, she thought, wiping her eyes.

Oh well, thought Topaz, who couldn't think of anything sad enough to feel remotely tearful. *At least by standing next to Octavia, I'm guaranteed to be in the shot. I can't wait to see myself on screen.*

Chapter Eight

Topaz decided not to be annoyed that Octavia had got the part of Hanky Girl in the film. 'Girl Next to Hanky Girl' wasn't quite what she had in mind, but it was better than 'Girl at the Back of the Crowd no one could see'.

'You'll definitely see a close-up of me!' Topaz told her mother. 'Sapphire says we'll be invited to the première.'

They didn't have to wait long for an envelope containing a stiff, white card edged with gold, inviting Topaz L'Amour and Guest to the film première at the multi-screen surround-sound Cosmic Cinema in Starbridge. Although Sapphire had said that the film probably wouldn't be released for months, a combination of Jake Lush being unable to get out of his air-conditioned trailer until mid-afternoon, because of late-night whisky-drinking sessions, and Vanessa Stratton turning up late to the location because she fancied *another* last-minute holiday, meant the film's release date was only weeks away. Already posters of Vanessa and Jake Lush were appearing around Starbridge.

The first time Topaz saw one of the posters she longed to get out her pen and scribble 'Also Starring Topaz L'Am♥ur!', but decided after the last poster incident, it probably wasn't a good idea.

In the days before the première, Topaz couldn't concentrate. She kept the invitation in her school bag, and during lessons she would carefully slip the stiff, white card into her textbook and stare longingly at it.

In fact, the only thing that threatened to spoil the occasion was the shoe problem.

As they hadn't had to find money for a new Palm Island wardrobe or passport, Topaz's mum had bought her a new dress for the première. The dress was short, pink and had a little flippy hem. It was lovely and Topaz had a pair of strappy silver sandals that would go perfectly with it. But until the night of the première, Topaz hadn't tried on her sandals since she'd thrown them in the back of her wardrobe at the end of last summer.

I've hardly worn them! thought Topaz in despair, as however much she scrunched up her feet it was obvious the sandals were too small. The straps cut into her ankles and her toes spilled over the end like escaping spiders. *I can't believe my feet have grown so much.*

Other than her dancing-shoes or trainers, the only shoes that fitted her were her clumpy black school shoes.

She persuaded herself that it didn't matter that her shoes were wrong as she would be sitting down at the première anyway, but now, waiting outside the flat for Parks to pick her up, she felt she might as well have arrows on her forehead pointing at her shoes.

The same stretch limousine with blacked out windows that had taken them to the airport to see Sapphire's mother pulled up outside the flats. Topaz looked around, hoping that someone – anyone – might see her getting in, but the street seemed unusually quiet, with only one other car coming slowly up Andromeda Road.

Just as Topaz was about to grab the limo's door handle, a voice shouted out, 'Topaz!' and she looked past the limo to see Sapphire waving out of the window of the ordinary-looking car behind.

'Who's in the car in front?' asked Topaz, clambering in the back of the car next to Sapphire and Ruby.

'My mother,' said Sapphire, rolling her eyes. 'Her

dress is so big it needed a car of its own. I've hardly seen her all day. She's been giving interviews, having her hair and make-up done. Where's your mum?'

'She's meeting us there,' said Topaz, thinking of her mum changing into her best dress in the toilets of one of the offices she cleaned.

Topaz glanced at her friends. Sapphire looked beautiful in a pale blue dress with little diamanté studded straps and Ruby looked lovely in her new glasses and a pale-green top and dark-green skirt.

'I look awful!' Topaz moaned.

'You look lovely!' said Sapphire. 'Your dress is so pretty.'

Topaz shook her head. 'My shoes are ruining everything!' she said, trying to pull her feet up to show her shoes and managing to kick the back of the driver's seat. 'Look!'

'They're fine,' said Ruby, not entirely convincingly. 'No one will notice your shoes.'

As the cars approached the cinema, they suddenly veered off the road into a side street and stopped.

'What's happening?' asked Topaz. 'Why have we stopped?'

'Mum has to be the last one to make an entrance,' said Sapphire. 'Parks will have noticed people are still arriving. We're just waiting for them to go in.'

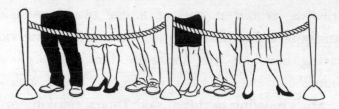

After waiting for a while, they overtook the limo and pulled out into the traffic.

My name will be in lights one day, thought Topaz, as she saw Vanessa Stratton's name stretched across the front of the cinema.

A row of policemen lined the road, holding back the crowd who were behind red velvet ropes. On the steps of the cinema, Topaz could see soap stars and pop stars and people who were no-one-knew-quite-why stars, smiling and waving for the cameras, striking a pose in outrageous dresses.

If only Kylie and Janice could see me now! thought Topaz as she looked out at the crowd, who were gawping in through the car windows as it pulled up alongside the red carpet. A man went to open the door and the bank of photographers raised their camera lenses.

This is it! thought Topaz excitedly, unclipping her seat belt. *This is what it's like to be a star!*

But as she got out of the car, her best smile stretched across her face, a disappointed moan rang out through the crowd. She heard someone shout, 'Save your film. It's nobody important!'

Topaz felt stung. *Nobody important!* she thought indignantly. *Just you wait! One day those shutters will be clicking for me!*

Suddenly, there was an explosion of light as cameras clicked and whirred and flashbulbs popped all around her.

'Over here!' someone called.

'Give us a wave!' yelled a voice.

For a moment, Topaz felt stunned and blinked furiously, trying to focus her eyes. As she did so, she saw Vanessa Stratton emerge from her limousine. She looked every inch the film star from her halo of blonde hair to her cream satin dress, the train of which tumbled out of the limo and on to the red carpet like a fast-flowing river.

As Parks helped arrange her dress, Vanessa Stratton noticed the familiar face of Scoop Mackenzie in the crowd. The last time she had seen him was at the airport when Sapphire had behaved so badly. Even though Scoop had given her a good write-up the following day, it was as well to make sure that he thought she was a good mother. She beckoned Sapphire over, and arm-in-arm, they walked down the red carpet as Topaz and Ruby were hurried into the cinema by burly security men.

'Any quotes for me?' asked Scoop as mother and daughter approached.

'Oh, I'm just a full-time mother with a part-time job as an actress,' purred Vanessa, still posing for the photographers. 'We're thrilled to be in the same film together, aren't we, darling?' She dug her manicured nails into Sapphire's arm as a reminder to smile for the cameras. Sapphire smiled and nodded.

As Vanessa and Sapphire entered the foyer and the doors of the cinema closed behind them, Rupert, Vanessa's assistant and Quentin, the PR man from Magnicolour Films, appeared from opposite directions. They seemed flustered.

'Jake Lush is missing,' hissed Quentin. 'We can't start without Jake.'

'Have you checked the local pubs?' said Rupert acidly. 'You know Jake likes a tipple or two.'

'Give him two minutes,' Vanessa said irritably. 'He'll be at the after-show party if he knows there are free drinks.'

Topaz, Ruby, Sapphire and Vanessa all stood in awkward silence.

Suddenly, there was a commotion at the cinema doors. A man seemed to be arguing with the doorman.

Vanessa sighed and rolled her eyes. 'It's probably Jake,' she said. 'He'll be drunk and stroppy. Someone let him in.'

The noise of banging and shouting on the door got

louder and louder until Vanessa couldn't bear it any longer.

'Oh for goodness' sake!' she hissed under her breath, but still smiling for the cameras. 'That noise is getting on my nerves. Let him in but keep him out of the photographs until he's sobered up.'

Quentin went to the door but before he could open it, a man who wasn't anything like a film star burst in and stood in the foyer, gasping for breath. As he loosened his tie, Topaz noticed he had several rings on his fingers and a chain around his neck.

'Don't close the door,' he called behind him. 'My wife and daughter are just behind me.'

Topaz could see someone standing on the steps and noticed the cameras flashing behind the glass doors. Whoever it was was *very* late and obviously determined to upstage Vanessa Stratton.

'You're late!' snapped Vanessa. 'Don't you know that I am supposed to be the last one through those doors?'

'Our car broke down on the way here,' said the man. 'Top of the range model, too! Fully loaded, leather seats and heated mirrors. I mean, you expect it of entry-level models, but not top of the range, do you?'

Topaz looked at the man. He seemed vaguely familiar.

'Who *are* you?' asked Vanessa, looking at the man as if a bad smell had just wafted under her nose.

The man handed a business card to Vanessa, who was so shocked she took it.

'Salesman of the year, three years running for Wunda Windows Double Glazing,' he said. 'I can do you a really good price on sealed PVC units if you order before the end of the month.'

Quentin from PR rushed off into the corner and began jabbering into his walkie-talkie. 'We've lost Lush and have a nutter in the foyer trying to sell Vanessa Stratton double glazing! *Do* something!'

Rupert clutched his head and moaned, 'This can't be happening!'

'Listen, you horrible little man,' snapped Vanessa, 'you have no right to be here so go or I'll have you thrown out!'

'You can't do that!' he said. 'I've got a ticket to this prèmiere. I'm Kevin Quaver and that's my daughter, Octavia. She's in your film.' The man gestured towards the door where with every pop of a flash gun, a girl with blonde hair could be seen waving.

Vanessa looked at Octavia playing to the photographers outside. She knew all about ambitious little starlets trying to grab the limelight. She'd been one herself.

'Get that little minx in here!' she hissed at Rupert, who hurried towards the door, only to hurry back almost immediately.

'She won't come!' he said. '*And* her mother threatened me with physical violence!'

Vanessa was furious. Picking up the train of her dress, she turned on her kitten heels and stormed outside where Octavia was pouting and preening in a tiny dress covered in silver sequins. Pauline Quaver could be heard telling Scoop Mackenzie, 'She's available to sing at weddings, bar mitzvahs and funerals – other professional engagements permitting, of course.'

'Get in here!' Vanessa hissed to Octavia, grabbing her wrist and hauling her into the foyer, whilst still managing to smile for the cameras. 'I know your game.'

Topaz glared at Octavia who stood with a self-satisfied grin plastered across her face.

'Your car didn't really break down, did it?' said Topaz. 'Your dad made that up just so you could make an entrance, didn't he?'

Octavia patted her blonde curls, smoothed down the silver sequins on her dress and shrugged. 'You've either got it or you haven't,' she said. 'And *you* haven't.'

Instead of sitting in the front row as Topaz had expected, they were directed to a row of seats at the back of the cinema. Lola was already sitting next to someone who could only be Ruby's father. His hair was so red it almost glowed. Several rows in front, Octavia, Pauline and Kevin Quaver were trying to get to their seats, annoying everyone with their late arrival.

A spotlight illuminated the stage, the audience hushed and Joshua P. Finkleberg walked on to wild clapping and cheering. Even though he was wearing a dinner jacket and bow-tie, he still had a baseball cap clamped to his head.

After a short speech where he thanked everyone involved in the film – including the lady that made the tea every morning – Joshua P. Finkleberg announced, 'Please welcome the stunning star of *A Heavenly Match*, the terrific, the talented, the extraordinarily beautiful Vanessa Stratton!'

Jake Lush was obviously still propping up a bar somewhere in Starbridge.

The audience rose to their feet as Vanessa Stratton swept down the aisle under a pink spotlight. She paused by a seat in the centre of the front circle, waved and the cinema went dark.

'She's not going to watch the film,' whispered Sapphire. 'She'll have slipped out to have a few champagne cocktails instead.'

'Your mum is amazing!' gasped Topaz.

'She's so glamorous!' whispered Ruby.

But not how mums are supposed to be! Sapphire thought to herself. Topaz could 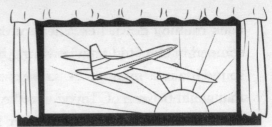 barely concentrate on the film as she waited for the final scene. *Her* scene. She fidgeted, she fiddled, she glanced at Sapphire during a scene where her mother kissed Jake Lush, but Sapphire's face remained expressionless.

I'd be so embarrassed if that was my mother kissing someone on screen, thought Topaz.

In the final tear-jerking scene, as Sister Ursula and Father O'Leary fly off into the sunset for the start of a new life together, hundreds of tearful orphans wave them goodbye.

Topaz nudged her mother and whispered, 'This is it! I'm going to appear any moment now. You won't be able to miss me!'

The camera panned high over a crowd of faces and a sea of waving hands. A shot of Ruby appeared on screen, her head buried in her hands, as if consumed with grief that her beloved Mother Ursula and Father O'Leary were leaving to be married. There was another crowd scene and a shot of a Bargain Basket delivery lorry that editing had failed to notice, before the camera zoomed in on Sapphire, staring into space, tears running down her pale face. Finally, the camera zoomed in close to Octavia waving her hanky, her tear-stained face a mixture of sadness and happiness. All that could be seen of Topaz was the blue tip of her left elbow as Octavia waved beside her.

The credits rolled, the curtain came down, Vanessa Stratton (who had slipped back into the cinema for the final scene) gave a gracious wave and the audience clapped enthusiastically.

Ruby's father, Rodney Ruddle, was delighted with his daughter's performance. 'You were so convincing!' he said. 'It was as if you really were upset. Your mother and I *knew* stage school would help you with your stage fright!'

Sapphire's mother was relieved that Sapphire seemed to have the makings of a good actress in her after all.

All that nonsense about becoming a doctor, she thought as she got back into the limo taking her to the after-show party at the Super Nova nightclub. *She's a natural!*

Topaz sat slumped in her seat crushed with disappointment. She'd spent weeks dreaming of being recognized. Of being pulled out of the crowd and catapulted to stardom. Out of all of them, she was the only one whose face had ended up on the cutting-room floor. They'd kept the Bargain Basket lorry in, but someone in editing had looked at the bit of film with her face on it and said, 'Cut that girl out.' Madame Catovia was right. Someone had looked at her and thought, *She doesn't have what it takes.*

'What bit were you in?' asked her mother as they left the cinema, passing the Quaver family who were asking if anyone wanted Octavia's autograph on the back of a Wunda Windows business card.

Topaz shrugged. 'Just a face in the crowd,' she said, trying not to cry until she had left the cinema. 'No one special.'

Chapter Nine

'Look at that!' Topaz growled as they waited in class for their chemistry lesson to begin. She pushed her copy of *Snapped!* magazine towards Ruby and Sapphire. A double-page spread featuring the première showed a picture of a smiling Vanessa Stratton holding hands with an angelic-looking Octavia Quaver.

'Whoever said the camera doesn't lie, lied,' said Topaz, scowling. 'No one would guess your mum was trying to pull the Evil One away from the photographers. They look like best friends!'

Ruby peered over the top of her glasses and looked at the photo-spread. 'You *are* in it, look!'

Topaz grabbed the magazine back and studied the picture. 'Where?' she said. 'I can't see me.'

Ruby pointed at the picture of Vanessa and Octavia and there, just poking out of the corner of the photograph, was a bit of white leg on the end of which was a clumpy black school shoe.

Topaz groaned. 'I guess that's what they call a bit-part actor,' she said. 'A bit of elbow, a bit of shoe.'

'You were just unlucky,' said Sapphire. 'If you hadn't been standing next to Octavia you might have been in shot.'

'And maybe Mr Finkleberg heard you call him a beardy-weirdy after all,' added Ruby, trying to be helpful.

Topaz sneezed. On top of the disappointment of only her elbow appearing in the film, she'd started to get a cold. Her nose was itchy and her throat felt sore and scratchy. She knew her friends were just trying to cheer her up, but nothing seemed to be helping. So many of Madame Catovia's predictions seemed to be coming true. Just when she thought she had a chance of being a star – or at least a starlet – something or someone would knock her back. Miss Diamond had told her that becoming a star wasn't just about talent, it was also about luck.

But am I a lucky sort of person? Topaz wondered, drawing horns on Octavia's picture and blacking out her teeth.

Was it bad luck that in the Starbridge Christmas

Show she'd been the back end of the pantomime horse, or good luck that Octavia had fallen down the stairs and not her? Was it good luck that she was chosen for the Zit Stop! campaign, or bad luck that she was the red-faced spotty 'before' picture and Octavia the smiling, clear-skinned 'after' girl? Was it good luck that she got the part of the voice-over in the Speedy Snax commercial, or bad luck that it meant she was waiting for Miss Diamond to find out and terminate her scholarship?

If I can't even decide if I'm lucky or not, how I am ever going to know if I'm talented? she thought glumly.

Miss Tuffstone, the science teacher, had been standing by Topaz's desk for some time before Topaz noticed.

No wonder we all call you Miss Toadstone, thought Topaz, looking up as the teacher looked down at her with bulging eyes and a double chin.

'Are you going to pay attention in this class, Topaz, or are you going to spend an hour practising your autograph and dreaming?' Miss Tuffstone puffed out her chest and looked even more toad-like.

Topaz looked at the front of her chemistry exercise book. Across the cover was scrawled *Topaz L'Am♥ur* over and over again. Miss Tuffstone whipped it out from under Topaz's nose.

'I do hope you've finished your chemistry

homework,' she said, moving on to the next desk.

Finished? thought Topaz. *I haven't even started it!*

Trudi Tuffstone looked at the class in front of her. Other than Sapphire Stratton, no one seemed the slightest bit interested in science. But today would be different. Today she was doing the first class demonstration since she'd accidentally blown her fingernails off during a practical lesson in the first term.

'Today we're going to look at oxidation!' she announced.

The class groaned. How would a lesson on oxidation help them get their name in lights?

Miss Tuffstone saw Topaz staring out of the window. *All that girl does is dream,* she thought to herself. Today she'd *make* Topaz concentrate. The demonstration was so simple, even Topaz could do it. Nothing could go wrong.

'Topaz,' called out Trudi Tuffstone, holding out a pair of safety goggles, 'I'd like you to help me with the experiment.'

Topaz was so busy staring out of the window, wondering whether she should tell Sapphire and Ruby about Madame Catovia's predictions, that she didn't hear Miss Tuffstone until Sapphire nudged her.

She walked to the bench, put on her goggles and the class giggled.

Miss Tuffstone stood behind the lab bench wearing goggles and gloves, turned on the gas and lit the Bunsen burner, which roared into life.

'I'm going to use a piece of magnesium ribbon to demonstrate oxidation!' Miss Tuffstone called out, over the roar of the Bunsen burner flame. The class began to chat amongst themselves as Miss Tuffstone cut a piece of ribbon from a coil, held it between forceps and, handing back the coil of ribbon to Topaz, said, 'Put that somewhere safe.

'Now, without looking directly into the flame, see the brilliance of the light when the ribbon ignites!' Miss Tuffstone gushed, excited at the thought of her own experiment. The class continued to ignore her.

She dipped the end of the ribbon into the flame and after a second, it crackled and fizzed and burst into a brilliant white light. It was like an indoor firework display. The class began to pay attention and 'Oohs' and 'Aahs' rang around the science lab. The ribbon disappeared into a pile of white ash on the bench below and the class gave her a round of applause. Trudi Tuffstone was enjoying herself. It wasn't often that she had the attention of the class.

Perhaps this *is what it's like to have an audience,* she

thought to herself. *Perhaps this is what it's like to perform under a spotlight!*

'Give us an encore!' someone shouted. 'Do it again!'

'Do a bigger bit!' someone else called out.

Miss Tuffstone took the coil of ribbon and pulled off an extra-long strip. Handing the coil back to Topaz, for a second time she lit the ribbon and the class watched the brilliant white light as the ribbon crackled like a powerful sparkler.

Topaz's nose itched. Her cold seemed to be getting worse. The white powder from the burning ribbon wasn't helping. Any minute now she was going to—

'ACHOO!' She let out an enormous sneeze, the force of which sent a piece of burning ribbon up into the air. The class watched with horrified fascination as the burning ribbon tumbled towards the pile of chemistry homework books on the desk, on top of which Topaz had left the coil of magnesium ribbon. There was a bang – a blinding white light and a tremendous fizzing noise – as flames began to engulf the pile of exercise books.

'Don't panic!' shouted Miss Tuffstone, clearly panicking as the books blazed away. 'Open a window!'

The class started coughing and spluttering as black smoke began to fill the science lab.

The fire alarm went off and the sprinklers in the ceiling began to pour water into the classroom, just as

Miss Tuffstone managed to throw a fire blanket over the burning books.

The class stood with dripping wet hair and clothes as Miss Tuffstone peeled back the fire blanket and stared at the pile of smouldering ash.

I am *lucky, after all!* thought Topaz, trying to suppress a smile. *Now Miss Toadstone will never find out I didn't do my homework.*

Trudi Tuffstone bent down beside her desk, picked up an exercise book, looked at the cover and waved it in the air.

'Topaz, you're lucky!' she said. 'Yours must have fallen off the desk. It's a bit wet but it survived the fire!'

Just as the sprinklers spluttered to a halt, Bob Feldspar burst into the lab, slipped on a puddle of water, skidded along the floor on his corduroy-clad bottom, before crashing, feet-first, against a desk.

'Everything all right, Trudi?' he asked, as several pupils helped him to his feet. 'Is anyone hurt, other than me?'

'No harm done!' said Miss Tuffstone. 'Topaz was just helping me with an experiment.'

'Well, if you're sure,' said the geography teacher, rubbing his bruised backside and looking at Topaz suspiciously.

Miss Tuffstone turned to Topaz, who was still

standing beside the desk staring at her rescued exercise book.

'What is it about you, Topaz L'Amour?' she hissed under her breath. 'Why do you always attract trouble?'

Chapter Ten

'Grumpy old Toadstone says I'm a troublemaker,' said Topaz, blowing her nose as they sat in Happy Al's Café after school.

'That's a bit unfair,' said Sapphire.

'Is it?' replied Topaz, thinking of the altered poster, Ruby's broken glasses, the maypole incident and the fire in the chemistry lab. 'I'm not so sure.'

The pay-phone on the wall began to ring. Al didn't attempt to answer it.

'I'll get that if you're busy,' called Ruby, getting up.

'Leave it!' snapped Al. 'It's no one I want to speak to.'

'I was only trying to help!' said Ruby, sitting back down and pulling a face.

The phone had rung several times whilst the girls had been in the café, drinking hot chocolate and talking about the look of panic on Miss Tuffstone's face as the chemistry books caught fire. Each time, Al had let the phone ring and carried on frying chips and buttering bread. The girls thought he wasn't answering the phone because he was busy, but it was now obvious that he was avoiding whoever was trying to get hold of him.

'Someone is keen to talk to him,' said Sapphire, as the telephone rang again and Al ignored it once more.

Suddenly, the door flew open, there was a smell of stale cigarette smoke and a small woman marched into the café, brandishing a mobile phone in her nicotine-stained hand. It was Zelma Flint.

Zelma stood in front of Al and waved her mobile phone in his face. 'Why did you put the phone down on me?' she demanded. 'I've been trying to speak to you for days. Why won't you answer my calls?'

Topaz remembered when, last term, Zelma Flint had burst into Miss Diamond's office, waving her mobile phone. Did everyone ignore Zelma's calls?

'There is *nothing* I have to say to you,' replied Al,

turning his back and fiddling with the steam nozzle on his Turbo Frother.

'But Al, sweetie, I have marvellous news!' Zelma began to move behind the counter but suddenly Al swung round and Zelma scuttled back to the safety of the other side.

'Petunia Bluff has been made commissioning editor at Pulsar Television and she wants to make a Christmas special of *Murder Mile*! As it's for Christmas, they'll need to start filming in a couple of weeks.'

Al stopped fiddling with the coffee machine. 'What's that got to do with me?' he asked suspiciously.

'What's that got to do with you?' rasped Zelma, throwing her hands in the air. 'You *are* Inspector 'Nosey' Parker, and *Murder Mile* can't exist without Nosey!'

Al remained silent as Zelma chattered on. 'Petunia said it was you or no one. People *loved* Nosey. People *loved* you! Petunia *adores* you!'

Pulsar Television didn't want me all those years ago when they sacked me! thought Al bitterly, as he wiped imaginary crumbs off the counter. Zelma Flint might be chasing him now, but she hadn't returned his calls when he was no longer a star and therefore not useful to her. He wanted nothing more to do with Zelma Flint or Pulsar Television.

'No!' he said. 'I won't do it!'

'Oh, well,' said Zelma, starting to use her phone. 'I'll

just have to get Jake Lush to play you as you were years ago.'

'But you said Petunia said it was me or no one!' said Al.

Zelma shrugged. 'Jake's very hot at the moment and as I couldn't get in touch with you, he's already on standby . . .'

'OK!' said Al suddenly. The thought of someone other than him playing Nosey Parker was too much to bear, especially Jake Lush. Jake Lush didn't even look like a detective. 'If I can get someone to run the café for a few days, I'll do it!'

'My mum might be able to do it!' said Topaz, jumping up. 'She was thinking of getting another job.'

Zelma was caught by surprise. She'd been so busy talking to Al, she hadn't noticed Topaz sitting in the café.

'Ah, Topaz!' she smiled, revealing a row of yellow peg-like teeth. 'I was just about to call you!'

Topaz didn't believe her for one moment. 'About the money for the Speedy Snax advert?' she asked.

Zelma ignored her and said, 'Now that Al has agreed to play Nosey Parker, I was going to offer you the part of Alice. It's a wonderful opportunity and there's no need for you to audition.'

Topaz tried not to show her excitement, but said in

what she hoped was a cool voice, 'What does Alice do?'

'What does Alice do?' repeated Zelma. 'The whole plot revolves around Alice!'

Topaz thought for a moment. She'd sworn never to work with Zelma Flint ever again, but then so had Al and *he'd* changed his mind.

'I'll need to clear it with Miss Diamond,' said Topaz. 'I didn't tell her about the Speedy Snax voice-over and I wish I had.'

Zelma smiled an oily yellow smile. 'Is that *really* necessary?' she said. 'Your part will be filmed at a weekend in and around the Starbridge Community Centre. You wouldn't even miss school. If you and I can come to some arrangement, there would be no need for her to know.'

Topaz took one step towards Zelma and said in a low voice, 'I *have* to clear it with the school. If you try to double-cross me, I'll tell Miss Diamond that I was in the Speedy Snax ad and that you didn't pay me enough even to buy a Noodle Burger. She'll make sure you *never* have anything to do with anyone from Precious Gems *ever* again!'

Zelma nodded. 'I'll be in touch,' she said.

'Miss Diamond will never let you play Alice!' said Ruby when Topaz sat down. 'Not after what she said last term.'

'You've already gone behind her back once with the

Speedy Snax voice-over,' said Sapphire. 'She'll definitely stop you taking the part.'

'I don't see why,' said Topaz. 'The Speedy Snax advert was last term, after all, and she's never asked what happened to the maypole or about the fire in chemistry. As far as Miss D is concerned, I've been the perfect pupil all term.'

'You will talk to her about the part, won't you?' said Ruby. 'You will listen to her advice?'

Topaz nodded and picked up her bag. 'Of course,' she said. 'I'm going back to school to see if I can catch her before she goes home. I might as well talk to her now.'

'She *must* be keen,' said Ruby as Topaz rushed out of the door and headed back towards school. 'She's left most of her hot chocolate.'

As Topaz was racing up Stellar Terrace towards the school, Miss Diamond was walking down it, her dress billowing around her like a galleon in full sail.

'Miss Diamond!' said Topaz breathlessly, 'I need to see you.'

'Ah, Topaz!' said the Headmistress. 'That's fortunate because I wanted to have a word with you.'

Topaz's stomach lurched. Had she found out about the Speedy Snax voice-over after all? She gave Miss Diamond a nervous smile and gulped.

'Don't look so worried!' laughed Miss Diamond. 'I just wanted to say how delighted I am that after our little chat last term, you've kept out of trouble and worked so hard. Well done!'

Topaz blew her nose. 'It's been very difficult, especially as so many people have told me I'll never be a star.'

Adelaide Diamond looked at the first-year in front of her. From the moment she had seen Topaz light up the stage at the auditions she'd known Topaz could be a star. But others at the school had not been so keen to give a scholarship to the girl from the wrong side of Starbridge with no experience. They were just waiting for her to fail and it wouldn't be beyond them to try and knock her confidence.

'Who's saying those things?' Miss Diamond demanded.

Topaz thought of Madame Catovia, Octavia Quaver and Joshua P. Finkleberg but just said, 'Oh, you know, people.'

'Listen, Topaz,' said Miss Diamond, 'show business is full of people out to knock your confidence, bring you down and make you feel small. Ignore them. Believe in yourself.'

'You mean,' said Topaz, 'that I should follow my dreams?'

Adelaide Diamond nodded vigorously. 'I do,' she said.

'So if people tell me not to do something, just ignore them and do it anyway?'

'Follow your instincts,' said the Headmistress. 'Don't let *anyone* stop you pursuing what you really want.'

'In other words, go for it?' said Topaz.

Adelaide Diamond smiled at Topaz. 'Succeeding in show business is about talent, luck *and* determination.'

Topaz thought about what Miss Diamond had just said. There was no need to ask her permission to play the part of Alice. 'Don't let anyone stop you,' Miss D had said. So she wouldn't.

'And what about you?' said Miss Diamond, 'What did you want to ask me?'

'Nothing,' said Topaz, her face a picture of puzzled innocence.

'Are you sure?' said Adelaide Diamond. 'I was convinced you said, "I need to see you".'

'Oh sorry,' said Topaz, shaking her head. 'I'm bunged up with cold. What I actually said was, "I'm *pleased* to see you".'

Chapter Eleven

'It'll be our little secret,' rasped Zelma Flint when Topaz phoned to accept the part of Alice.

'She'll know when she sees me on television!' said Topaz, who was beginning to have second thoughts about not telling Miss Diamond. 'I don't see how we can keep it quiet.'

'There's absolutely nothing to worry about,' Zelma assured her. 'I'll ask Jack to arrange transport to the location. Have you got a chaperone?'

'Mum's working in Al's Café,' said Topaz. 'I could go on my own.'

'Go on your own!' Zelma spluttered. 'At your age! I'd never work in this town again if I allowed that. I'll tell Jack to arrange transport *and* a chaperone.'

'What about a script?' Topaz asked. 'Who will send me a script?'

'Must go!' said Zelma, putting the phone down.

On the morning of the filming Topaz was up bright and very early, waiting at the entrance to the flats on Andromeda Road for a large shiny black car to whisk her off to the film set. It wasn't quite the same as a film studio sending a private jet as they did for Vanessa Stratton, but surely it would be a limousine, at the very least? Alice was obviously a *very* important part. Zelma had said that the entire plot revolved around Alice. It was a bit worrying that no one had sent her a script, but at least that meant she hadn't had to spend hours learning lines.

Perhaps they want me to improvise, she thought.

Topaz looked at her watch. The limo was late. Her stomach rumbled and she wondered whether she could ask the car to stop at Happy Al's, where her mum would be cooking breakfasts. Lola Love had been only too happy to get a few days' work in the café, even though Al had left strict instructions that she mustn't touch the Turbo Frother and must only make coffee with the kettle.

Lola had suggested that they might be able to have a little summer holiday with the extra money, but Topaz had been disappointed when her mother had said that they still wouldn't be able to afford a trip to Whoosh Water World, but could manage a few days in a caravan at Boddington Sands.

A rusty red banger spluttered its way up Andromeda Road, leaving a trail of thick black smoke behind it. It came to a stop and children with runny noses stared out of the back windows.

A flustered woman leaned out of the window and shrieked, 'You Alice?'

Topaz shook her head and continued to look down the road for her shiny chauffeur-driven limousine.

'You sure you're not Alice?' shouted the woman. 'I'm supposed to be chaperoning an Alice to a filming.'

Topaz stared at the rust-bucket and the snotty-nosed children, and realized with disappointment that *this* was the transport that Zelma Flint had organized for her.

'It's me,' said Topaz, getting in the back, trying to shrink away from the children who not only had runny noses but sticky fingers. 'I'm playing the part of a girl called Alice.'

'Then why didn't you say so?' said the woman as the car lunged forward before lurching and bucking its way down the street, its exhaust backfiring like a starting pistol.

It was already stiflingly hot but the window on her side didn't seem to open so Topaz sat huddled in the corner, giving the children 'touch me and I'll scream' type looks. Every so often she noticed a fluorescent orange arrow saying Film Unit pinned to a lamppost. Eventually the car pulled into a road blocked off by a line of traffic cones. In the distance, people with clipboards were scurrying about.

'I'll drop you here,' said the woman. 'I can't stay, I've got to get the weekly shop in. You look like you can take care of yourself.'

Topaz was about to protest that a chaperone was supposed to stay with her all day and even organize her breakfast, but decided the sooner she was out of the rust-bucket and away from the snivelling runny-nosed, sticky-fingered children, the better.

'Thank you,' she said, scrambling out of the car and gulping a lungful of fresh air.

She could hear the car backfiring as she walked towards the collection of caravans, camper vans, generator trucks and tents lining the road outside the Starbridge Community Centre.

'Topaz L'Amour. I'm playing Alice,' she said to a woman with a clipboard and a walkie-talkie.

The woman flicked over several pages of notes before ordering, 'Yours is the first scene to be shot. First stop: Wardrobe.'

'I haven't got a script,' said Topaz.

The woman shrugged and pointed at an old bus with Clapperboard Catering written down the side. 'Get some breakfast after you've been to wardrobe.'

The electricity generator trucks hummed as Topaz picked her way over the electric cables snaking across the ground. She couldn't see anything with a sign saying 'Wardrobe' and there didn't seem anyone to ask.

A shrill voice floated across the air. 'Octavia Quaver. I'm playing Abigail. Where's my dressing room?'

As Topaz rounded the corner, there, standing at the back of a truck groaning with clothes rails, was Octavia. Topaz didn't feel surprised or disappointed. Somehow she *expected* to see Octavia.

'Hello, Octavia,' she said. 'I'm playing the part of Alice.'

Octavia turned round and glared at Topaz. 'Part!' she sneered. 'You're nothing more than a glorified extra. Even Melody turned the part of Alice down.'

A woman in the back of the truck leaned out and handed Octavia a lovely purple skirt, a lilac top and a pair of snazzy trainers and said, 'Trailer 4B. Hair and make-up will be waiting for you.'

Octavia didn't even say thank you. She just took the clothes and sauntered off.

Topaz looked up at the wardrobe lady. 'Topaz L'Amour and I'm playing Alice.'

She was sure the woman said 'Hard luck' under her

breath before she disappeared into the truck and came back with what looked like a massive grey blanket.

'Here we are. Catch!' said the woman, dropping the bundle over the edge of the truck. It was so heavy, Topaz staggered backwards as she tried to catch it.

'It's a duffle-coat!' Topaz gasped, as a pair of black wellingtons came flying out of the truck. 'It's boiling hot! Who wears a duffle-coat and wellies on a hot day?'

'You do,' said the wardrobe mistress. 'It's *supposed* to be Christmas Day.'

Remembering what Octavia had said, Topaz asked, 'Which dressing room do I use?'

'Use the toilets in the community centre,' said the woman.

'And hair and make-up?' Topaz asked weakly.

'No need for either,' said the wardrobe mistress tossing a red hat and scarf at Topaz before looking past her and shouting, 'Next!'

Topaz stood in the stifling heat, wearing a hat and scarf which itched, a thick winter coat which was too big and wellies which were too small. No one seemed to be telling her what to do or where to go. Everyone seemed busy, rushing around being important, moving equipment, waving clipboards or barking instructions into walkie-talkies. For a fleeting moment, she wished that she had a chaperone – any chaperone – even the red-faced woman with the snotty-nosed children.

She queued up outside the Clapperboard Catering bus and got a greasy bacon sandwich and a cup of strong, stewed tea in a plastic cup.

'Drab suits you!' said Octavia sarcastically as she breezed past, wiggling her hips in her little purple outfit. 'Come and watch *my* scene when you've finished yours!'

Topaz looked at the tea and the sandwich and tossed them in the nearest bin. Suddenly she had no appetite.

'Nosey and Alice to set!' boomed a voice. 'Nosey and Alice to set!'

Nosey appeared from a caravan with a gold star on the door. Despite being billed as the star, he was still grumpy.

'I hope your mum hasn't touched the Turbo Frother,' he said gruffly when he saw Topaz. 'I'll ring her as soon as this scene is over, just to make sure.'

In the blazing sun, Topaz trudged after Al over the playing field next to the community centre. The hat and scarf itched, her wellies pinched her feet and the duffle-coat weighed a ton. A man with a hose was watering a patch of grass between the goal posts until it was swimming with water and mud. Men and women with black T-shirts stood around holding cameras, lights and microphones.

A tall man with glossy black hair walked over.

'Raj Singh,' said the director, shaking Al's hand. 'Great to be working with you. Let's see if we can get *Murder Mile* back on our screens. If the special goes well, there's a possibility Pulsar might commission a new series!'

Al nodded and tried not to look too excited.

'OK!' said Raj. 'There's no need for a run-through. Let's get some film in the can!'

Topaz looked confused. 'I'm not actually sure what I'm supposed to be doing,' she said. 'I'm afraid I didn't get a script and no one I ask seems to have one either.'

Raj Singh stared at her. 'You're playing Alice, right?'

Topaz nodded enthusiastically.

'Then you don't need a script.'

'Oh!' said Topaz. 'You mean you want me to improvise?'

Raj Singh looked irritated. 'Improvise! Don't you know *anything* about the part you're playing?'

Topaz looked around her. The sound man, the camera woman, the lighting man and people with clipboards and stopwatches were staring at her. Happy Al was looking even more unhappy than usual. Worst of all, at the back of the crowd she could just see Octavia who had come to watch the taping.

'I'm – I'm playing the part of Alice,' Topaz stuttered. 'I'm in the first scene! My agent said the whole plot revolves around Alice.'

She noticed Octavia smirking and heard her giggle.

Raj Singh clasped his forehead. 'Someone tell her!'

'Tell me what?' asked Topaz.

A woman appeared at her side. 'There's no need for a script,' she said. 'You have a non-speaking part. Alice is found on Christmas Day, dead between goalposts in a field. *That's* the crime Nosey Parker has to solve.'

Chapter Twelve

No wonder Melody Sharp turned the part down and Zelma Flint told me not to worry about being seen on telly, seethed Topaz as she sat between the goalposts in the muddy field waiting for the cameras to roll. *No one will see me!*

There was no way she had jeopardized her scholarship, sat in the back of a rusty car with snotty children, stood in a heavy winter coat in boiling sunshine, walked across a muddy field in tight wellingtons *and* put up with Octavia's smirking, just to be a faceless dead body covered in mud. During her first term at Precious Gems, Pearl Wong, the senior pupil who had looked after the newcomers, had told her that however small a part, you could always, somehow, make it your own.

I'll make this dead body a dead body to remember, she thought as Raj Singh called out, 'Settle down, please. Take your positions.'

Topaz lay face down in the mud and waited.

'Lights, camera, relax and . . . ACTION!' shouted Raj Singh.

As the clapperboard snapped shut, Topaz leaned her head to one side and made a huge sighing noise.

'Cut!' shouted the director. 'What do you think you're doing?'

Topaz pulled herself up and rested on her elbows. 'I'm *trying* to let the audience know that I'm dying,' she said. 'I'm trying to set the scene!'

Raj Singh slapped his hand against his head. 'You're not dying,' he said through gritted teeth. 'You're already DEAD!'

'I think it might help me if I knew *how* I died.' said Topaz. 'At school they always tell us to get to know the character we're playing.'

Raj Singh looked as if he might explode at any minute. He didn't want to direct this low budget remake of an old show for television. He wanted to direct movies where beautiful girls wearing jewel-covered saris danced in flower gardens. Instead he was in a muddy field in Starbridge trying to tell some stage school kid in a duffle-coat how to play a dead body.

Raj Singh raised his voice. 'You don't *need* to get into

the character. There is no character. The character is found dead in a field. We don't know why. We have to find out. THAT IS THE POINT OF THE PROGRAMME!' He was shrieking by now and raising his fists in the air.

Topaz wanted to point out that if he read the script all the way through to the end he would find out how she had died and could tell her, but the look on his face told her it was better to keep quiet.

'Sorry,' she said, flopping back down into the mud. 'I'll play dead.'

Barely had the signal been given to start the cameras rolling again than the director screamed, 'Cut!'

'Your leg was twitching,' he said looming over her. '*Why* was your leg twitching?'

'Nerves twitch for a bit after you're dead,' said Topaz. 'We learnt that in science. I thought it would make the body seem more realistic.'

'This is a TV series!' screamed the director. 'It's not real life. *I'm* not interested in real life. The viewers aren't interested in real life. Now. Again.'

The lights shone, the microphone hovered and the cameras rolled.

'Action!'

'Sorry!' said Topaz, sitting up as the crowd groaned. 'The mud has got in my mouth. Can I just have a good cough first?'

'No!' growled the director. 'Get on with it.'

Just as Topaz was about to lie in the mud again, she felt the skin on the back of her hand crawl and she noticed a worm wriggling across her hand. 'ARGHHH!' she yelled, flapping her hands in the air and sending mud splattering all over Raj Singh's face. 'It's a worm!'

Raj Singh wiped his muddy face on his sleeve. He wagged a finger at Topaz and said in a menacing voice, 'You have one chance, young lady. One chance to lie still in that mud and play dead or you are off the set! Do you understand?'

Topaz nodded. There was still mud up her nose and the worm was still too close for comfort, but she daren't move. She slumped forward into the mud, the director told everyone to settle down, someone called 'Action!' and above her she could hear Happy Al say, 'It takes years of experience to know *that* is a dead body.'

'Cut!' a voice yelled.

'Thank you!' shouted another. 'Scene one over. Everyone take five!'

Topaz tried to sit up but her duffle-coat was stiff with wet mud and her wellies were full of water.

'Help!' she called through a mouthful of mud. 'I'm stuck.'

No one came and she became worried that even more worms would appear, so eventually she managed to haul herself to her feet. The field was empty. The cameras, lights and microphones had gone. She trudged back to the Community Centre with slow, painful steps.

Octavia was right, she thought. *I wasn't anything more than a glorified extra.*

The inside of the community centre had been transformed to look like a living room, although most living rooms didn't have cameras and lights around the edges and yards of electric cable snaking across the floor. There was a false wall with a pretend front door which had been left open. A rather sorry-looking Christmas tree sat in the corner with only half its fairy lights working and a few badly wrapped presents underneath. Octavia was sitting on the arm of the sofa patting her blonde curls and smiling at the camera men whilst Al paced up and down, rehearsing his lines. A woman who Topaz vaguely recognized from a washing powder advert was playing the part of Abigail and Alice's mother.

It's probably just as well no one could see me, thought Topaz, flicking the mud out of her nails. *I don't think I could bear to spend the summer holidays worrying about Miss D finding out about the Speedy Snax advert* and *this!*

'Positions, please!' shouted Raj Singh as he walked on to the set.

Al and the washing powder woman disappeared behind the false wall and Octavia sat on the sofa pretending to read a magazine.

'Relax, ready and . . . Action!' called the director.

Inspector 'Nosey' Parker walked through the door shouting, 'Hello! Is there anyone at home?'

'Who are you?' shrieked Abigail, throwing her magazine into the air in surprise.

'Police,' said Inspector 'Nosey' Parker gruffly. 'Sorry to startle you. Are you Abigail?'

Abigail nodded.

The woman playing the girls' mother entered the room and said dramatically, 'Inspector! Is it bad news? Is it about Alice? She's been missing for days!'

'Nosey' Parker nodded gravely. 'I'm afraid it's not the sort of Christmas present you were hoping for, ma'am.'

He turned to Abigail who was sitting wide-eyed on the sofa. 'I'd like a few moments alone with your mother. Could you leave us?'

'NO!' shrieked a voice. 'Stay *right* where you are!'

'CUT!' shouted Raj Singh.

The crowd watching the shoot parted and a furious Pauline Quaver, wearing a shiny purple tracksuit, stomped on to the set, wagging a podgy pale finger at the director. Pauline Quaver's hands always reminded Topaz of uncooked sausages.

'My daughter had been promised that she would be in this scene from start to finish. Where in the script did it have her leaving the set after three words and a nod of the head?' Pauline's eyes were blazing and her head looked as if it might start spinning with rage at any moment.

A man with a clipboard hurried over and said, 'We had a last-minute rewrite. The executives at Pulsar TV didn't feel it appropriate that a young girl remain in the room to hear such bad news about her beloved sister.'

Beloved sister! thought Topaz sourly. *Even if she was my sister, I wouldn't love Octavia!*

Pauline Quaver took a step forward and stood eyeball-to-eyeball with the clipboard man, who had now started to shake. 'I don't *care* what you think is appropriate. What is not appropriate is that my daughter has said only one line and is out of the scene!' Pauline Quaver was shouting so loudly, Clipboard Man's hair was blown backwards. 'Are you saying she plays no further part in this scene?'

The man flicked nervously through his notes before stuttering, 'Only as "sound of sobbing from bedroom".'

'You don't know what you're doing!' bellowed Pauline Quaver at the director. 'You don't even recognize star talent!'

Octavia, who had been watching from the sofa, jumped up and shrieked, 'Call yourself a director! You're just an amateur! I've worked with Joshua P. Finkleberg. *You* couldn't even direct a school play!'

'ENOUGH!' Raj Singh bellowed, grabbing a microphone stand and brandishing it at Pauline Quaver. 'You are the worst example of a pushy stage school mother and daughter I have *ever* come across and I've come across hundreds!'

Pauline Quaver turned scarlet. 'How dare you speak to me like that!' she said. 'Who do you think you are?'

Raj Singh held the microphone stand in front of him like a spear. 'I, madam, am the director. This is *my* set, *my* production and *you* will do what I say.'

Pauline Quaver put her hands on her hips and sneered. 'Oh yeah? And how are you going to make me?'

A twisted smile crept across the director's face. 'Your daughter is fired! I want you both to leave the set now. We'll recast Abigail.'

Pauline Quaver stood open-mouthed. 'You can't do that!' she gasped. 'You can't sack Octavia!'

'Oh yes, I can,' said Raj Singh. 'I've just done it. Now get off my set!'

Topaz was standing wide-eyed at the edge of the set.

'You!' Raj Singh shouted, pointing at Topaz. 'You

can play your own sister. No one will recognize you when you're not covered in mud and a duffle-coat! Get to wardrobe and find yourself something to wear.'

Topaz couldn't believe her luck. She didn't just have one part in *Murder Mile*, she had two! She'd worry about how to tell Miss Diamond another day.

A woman with a clipboard approached. 'Hair and make-up are waiting for you, Miss L'Amour!' she said. 'Trailer 4B. I'll show you the way.'

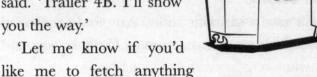

'Let me know if you'd like me to fetch anything from Clapperboard Catering,' said someone else.

Topaz sat in the trailer whilst the hair and make-up team fussed about, primping this, painting that. Someone from wardrobe delivered the lilac outfit Octavia had been wearing earlier. When Topaz emerged from the trailer she was unrecognizable as the girl in the mud-covered duffle coat.

'Hard luck!' said Topaz sarcastically as she passed Octavia, sitting at the side of the set sobbing. Her mother was barking into her mobile phone, 'We'll sue Pulsar TV for every penny they have!'

'You're laughing now, but you'll never be a star,' Octavia shouted through her tears. 'You just don't have what it takes and your acting is pants!'

Topaz stopped in her tracks and spun round. 'What did you just say?' she said to Octavia.

'I said, you're laughing now, but you'll never be a star. You just don't have what it takes and your acting is pants!'

Octavia's eyes glittered with anger. Eyes that Topaz had looked into when she'd last heard those same words.

'It was you!' Topaz gasped. '*You* were the evil Madame Catovia.'

Octavia gave a sarcastic snort. 'Any fool could work out that Catovia was an anagram of Octavia,' she said. 'Except you.'

Topaz glared at Octavia. And then she began to laugh. She laughed until her sides ached and tears rolled down her face. She'd spent all term worrying that Madame Catovia really could see into the future and predict that she'd never be a star, and all that time it had been the evil, jealous, scheming Octavia, dressed up as an old woman.

'What are you laughing at?' said Octavia indignantly.

'You!' said Topaz. 'I'm laughing at you! You're pathetic, Octavia Quaver!'

'I'll tell my mum to get you to stop!' whined Octavia. 'She won't let you laugh at me!'

'The same mum who got you sacked from the film

set?' asked Topaz, nodding at Pauline Quaver who was still bellowing into her phone.

Raj Singh approached. 'Just to let you know we've decided to write more lines for Abigail,' he said. 'We're going to really beef up her part. You'll be on set for the entire scene and maybe some others later on. Now we've rewritten it I think you'll find Abigail is a really great role.'

Topaz smiled sweetly at Octavia, who was as white as a sheet.

'Just face it, Octavia,' she said. 'You've either got it or you haven't, and thanks to you and your mum, I've got it!'

'Everyone on set!' called a voice over a loud-hailer. People started rushing about, muttering into walkie-talkies, adjusting camera angles, checking sound levels. Happy Al and the washing powder woman were already on set, practising their lines. Topaz walked on to the set and sat on the sofa, waiting to begin, and as she did so, huge spotlights burst into life, flooding the scene with a brilliant white light.

'Topaz, this is your moment, are you ready?' called out Raj Singh as a woman stood at the side of the set holding a clapperboard.

Topaz nodded.

As the woman shouted 'Action!' and the clapperboard snapped shut, Topaz knew without any doubt that all the struggles, disappointments and hard work were worth it for this moment. The moment she was about to become a star.

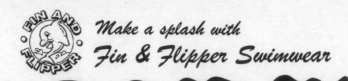

Another sparkling Topaz production!

Topaz Steals the Show
by Helen Bailey

Topaz L'Amour is ecstatic – she's won a place at Precious Gems Stage School! But in the world of show business, learning to tap dance on the bathroom floor with drawing pins in your trainers counts for nothing. Topaz quickly learns that life at stage school is hard work.

And she doesn't just have to cope with lack of training. Her rival, the scheming and ambitious Octavia Quaver from Rhapsody's Theatre Academy, is doing her best to steal the limelight . . .

Another sparkling Topaz production!

Topaz Takes a Chance
by Helen Bailey

Flushed with her success in the Starbridge Christmas show, Topaz asks Adelaide Diamond, Headmistress of Precious Gems, if she can appear in advertisements. And she's about to audition for her first big break: the key role in the Zit Stop! advertising campaign.

But the path to fame and fortune is never smooth – particularly when blocked by arch-rival Octavia Quaver from Rhapsody's Theatre Academy . . .